GW00801709

NIGHTMARES

Also published by Poolbeg

Shiver!

Chiller

NIGHTMARES

Terrifying Tales from Beyond the Grave

POOLBEG

Published 1996
by Poolbeg Press Ltd
123 Baldoyle Industrial Estate
Dublin 13, Ireland

"The Poster" © JH Brennan 1996
"A Terrible Mistake" © Maeve Friel 1996
"Knick-Knock" © Michael Carroll 1996
"The Beast" © Ivy Bannister 1996
"Sun Day" © Michael Scott 1996
"The Land Of My Dreams" © Eileen Dunlop 1996
"The Canal" © Hugh Scott 1996
"Nightmare" © Morgan Llywelyn 1996
"The Worm Turns" © Vincent Banville 1996
"Rainbow Dreaming" © Soinbhe Lally 1996
"The Final Bust" © Tom Richards 1996
"The Devil Looks After His Own" © 1996
"The Thirteenth Floor" © 1996

The moral right of the author has been asserted.

A catalogue record for this book is available from the British Library.

ISBN 1 85371 632 4

Cover illustration by PJ Lynch
Cover design by Poolbeg Group Services Ltd
Set by Poolbeg Group Services Ltd in Goudy 11/14
Printed by The Guernsey Press Ltd,
Vale, Guernsey, Channel Islands.

Contents

THE POSTER
J H Brennan

Donny got the poster as part of a blind swap deal set up by Harry Foster.

Harry, who had the makings of a wide boy, persuaded maybe a dozen kids at Chopra Elementary to put together bundles of junk they didn't need and exchange them via Harry. It was a dumb deal, but sort of appealing. You just never knew whether the bundle you got might have the one thing you wanted most in all the world . . . a Roman coin . . . an old *Blur* single . . . a pair of *Marvin the Martian* socks . . .

It never happened of course, but you kept hoping. Meanwhile, Harry collected 50p each time a bundle changed hands.

Donny Beck opened his latest bundle (his third – how's that for optimism?) in the privacy of his room, partly because he always went up to his room when he came home from school, partly because he didn't want anybody to see what sort of junk he'd acquired. Most of it was rubbish, just as he'd suspected, but between a threadbare scarf and a battery-driven bus that didn't run, he came across the poster.

It was a film poster, advertising an old horror flick called

Child's Play. Donny had never seen the film. His parents wouldn't let him watch horror flicks and there'd been a lot of controversy about that one. But he knew what it was about because of all the talk. *Child's Play* was about a doll called Chuckie that came to life and murdered people.

The poster showed Chuckie, a cheerful little fellow with bright red hair, walking away from a large cabin trunk. He carried a bloodstained knife so long it was almost a sword. In the trunk you could see bits of a dismembered body and a severed human head. The head was turned away, but from the side it looked a bit like Tommy Farr, which was a bonus of sorts. Chuckie was smiling.

Donny's eyes lit up as he looked at it. The poster was really cool. It was just the right size for a space he happened to have on his bedroom wall. He could look at it while lying tucked up warm in bed and it would have the added benefit of driving his parents ape-shit since they disapproved so much of film violence.

Donny started rummaging in his cupboard for the Bluetac.

That night, Donny woke with a start. He must have been dreaming because his heart was pounding in his chest. But more than that, he had the weird feeling that somebody was in his room.

He pushed himself upright in the bed. He knew nobody was in his room, of course. His parents had both refused to step across the threshold until he cleaned it. He'd thrown his sister, Aileen, out often enough for her to take the hint. Nobody came into his room any more, especially while he was sleeping.

All the same, the weird feeling persisted.

Donny held his breath and listened. For a fraction of a

second he thought he heard a gentle rustle, like a particularly quiet mouse, but then there was silence. The silence stretched so long he came to the conclusion he'd imagined the rustling.

There was a light coming from the wall opposite his bed.

Donny stared towards it, frowning. It wasn't particularly bright – much like a patch of moonlight really, except the window was in the wrong place to reflect on that part of the wall wherever the moon might be. So where was the light coming from?

After a minute it struck him. It was the poster! The poster he'd stuck up earlier was glowing gently.

Donny's face lit up in a delighted smile. His new poster was actually *luminous*! That was really, *really* cool. He'd never seen a luminous movie poster before. But when you thought of it, a luminous poster was ideal for a horror movie. Now he knew what it was, he realised how well the artist had done. The glow was a hideously eerie green.

Still smiling, Donny lay back down and went to sleep.

The minute he reached school next day, Peter Flynn waylaid him to tell him about Tommy Farr. "Disappeared!" Pete said dramatically.

"What do you mean, 'disappeared'?" asked Donny. Tommy wasn't a particular friend, but they were both in the same class, so he was interested.

"Gone," Pete said, spreading his hands palm upwards. "Missing. Not here any more. The police were round first thing this morning asking questions. I expect they'll want to talk to you since you knew him."

Harry Foster sauntered up. "You telling him about Tommy?"

Pete nodded. "Hear anything more?"

Harry shook his head. "Naw. Peggy Ash says they're dragging the pond in the old quarry, but I don't believe her."

"Do you think he's run away from home?" Donny asked.

"Wouldn't surprise me," Peter Flynn said soberly. "You know his mother's put a blue rinse through her hair?"

"I tell you what," Harry Foster said, "if he's run away from home he never said a thing to me, and I saw him yesterday for his trade-in bundle." He stopped and looked at Donny. "Hey, maybe there's a clue in it! That was the bundle I gave to you!"

The police did talk to Donny Beck, but weren't especially interested in his trade-in bundle. In fact they weren't especially interested in anything he had to say, which wasn't much. He had the idea the inquiries were purely routine. Presumably, if you were a policeman you had to deal with quite a lot of kids running away from home. Tommy Farr was just one more.

The police interview meant he was home late so he arrived just as his father was coming back from the early shift. They both went off for a quick game of soccer. Between that and tea and homework, he didn't get near his room until he was actually going to bed.

He noticed the poster at once. Chuckie had turned round.

Donny stared. The poster used artwork rather than a still from the film and the artwork, in many ways, was crude. The cabin trunk was drawn with bold, thick lines. The colourings of the dismembered body were stark, with lots of red for blood. But Chuckie had been drawn differently, with far more detail, so that it looked almost like a photographic rendition. The result was that the doll and its bloodstained knife was very much the focus of the poster.

And Donny would have sworn the doll had turned round.

He stood staring at the poster and frowning, trying to remember exactly how it looked when he stuck it up. The best picture he could bring to mind was of the trunk to the left of the scene and Chuckie a little right of centre, walking away. That was the important part. He was *walking away*. That meant he was *facing* away.

Except now he wasn't. The trunk was still in the same place. Chuckie was still in the same place. But now Chuckie had turned his head so he was looking back at the trunk. Donny was certain he hadn't been like that before.

Nearly certain.

The thing was, Chuckie *couldn't* have turned his head because Chuckie was just ink on paper. It had to be Donny's memory. It had to be that the first time Donny looked he'd made a mistake. He'd sort of assumed that since Chuckie was *walking* away from the trunk, he had to be *looking* away from the trunk. It was what you'd expect, so his mind played a little trick to make sure that was what he got. Simple explanation.

When Donny climbed into bed and killed the light, he could see the faint moonlight glow of the poster on the wall opposite his bed. He lay looking at it for a long time before he fell asleep.

The next morning Chuckie was walking towards the trunk.

Donny found it tricky to concentrate on his school work that day. Right through the morning he found himself thinking about the poster. Whatever about the business of

5

the way the doll was facing, he *knew* when he first put up the poster, Chuckie had definitely been walking away from the trunk. There was no question in his mind about that. Chuckie was on the right of the trunk, walking right. Now he was on the right of the trunk, walking left.

His grin seemed a little wider, too.

But even while he was thinking this, Donny was also thinking it couldn't be true. Little red-haired guys in pictures didn't just turn around. They couldn't. They weren't real.

A way-out thought struck him. In the movie, Chuckie was a doll that came to life. Maybe the movie people had created a special-effects poster, using holograms or something, that made it look as if Chuckie was coming to life in the poster as well! Maybe they fixed it so he seemed to move about.

Donny suddenly remembered a badge he'd once got out of a cornflakes packet. It had a picture of a zebra that turned into a lion when you looked at it from a different direction. You twisted the badge back and forth and the pictures flipped – zebra, lion, lion, zebra. The surface of the badge was sort of ridged and the picture quality wasn't up to much, but what did you expect free in a packet of cornflakes? Movie people had a bundle of money. They could afford to make up a poster with the very best special effects. It glowed in the dark, didn't it? Maybe it moved as well.

Or maybe Aileen switched posters on him in the night!

That thought hit him like a rollercoaster. It made a lot more sense than the special effects idea. Aileen was younger than he was, at an age when kids were big into practical jokes. She'd always resented the fact that he wouldn't let her come into his room when she wanted. Maybe this was her way of getting even.

The more he thought about it, the more sense it made. There were a couple of different posters – maybe more than a couple – and somehow Aileen had got hold of them. Switch one for the other and anybody who didn't know would think the picture on the poster had changed. It *had* to be Aileen. It would even make sense of the little rustling noise he kept hearing in the night. It was Aileen, creeping about the room in the dark!

Donny was so certain he'd solved the mystery of the poster that he relaxed. That afternoon was games and, by the middle of the soccer practice, he'd managed to forget it altogether.

Aileen denied everything. She denied having any movie posters (except for one of Brad Pitt, whom she planned to marry). She denied having even *seen* his stupid poster or come into his rotten smelly room, let alone messed around with anything in it. She denied leaving her own room, or waking up in the night, or playing practical jokes, or wanting to get even, or anything else that made her seem even a little less saintly than Mother Teresa.

To his surprise, Donny found he believed her. He'd always known when she was lying and he didn't think she was lying now.

Chuckie had moved closer to the trunk.

This time Donny didn't doubt his memory, didn't for a moment think he was looking at some sophisticated print effect. Chuckie moved. The damn doll in the picture moved. It was now left of centre by an inch or two, facing the trunk and grinning a big cheesy grin that was definitely wider than it had been before. The knife was no longer just bloodstained. It was now actually *dripping blood*. There was a little pool beside Chuckie's foot.

Donny felt his neck crawl.

He took time out to fight with himself just a little longer. Pictures couldn't move. He was imagining it. His sister . . . the special effects movie people . . . Eventually he let go of it all and faced the facts as squarely as he faced the poster. Somehow, the thing in the poster was able to move. Somehow it had turned its head, then twisted right around, then started walking towards the trunk. Grinning.

For a moment he considered asking his folks if he could sleep in their room tonight, but he knew it was a really stupid idea. Even when he was a little kid, he'd made a fuss about having a room of his own, and he'd got one just as soon as he was big enough. He had the idea his parents were delighted to have him out of theirs. There was no way he could ask to share with Aileen. He was far too old for that now even if she'd let him. And she wouldn't. Aileen, who thought she should be able to walk into anybody else's room when she wanted, went ballistic if anybody came within a hundred yards of hers. He was stuck with sleeping in his own room.

But he was damned if he was sleeping in the same room as the poster. He reached up and ripped it from the wall. Little blobs of Bluetac rolled and bounced across the floor. Donny rolled the poster tightly, picture side inwards, used one remaining blob of Bluetac to stick it tight, then pushed it into the back of his cupboard.

There was a key in the lock that he hadn't used in years, but something made him use it now. With the poster out of sight and his cupboard locked, he felt easier. All the same he left the light on when he went to bed. It was still on when he fell asleep.

Donny woke in darkness. The faint glow opposite his bed told him at once the poster was back on the wall.

8

He jerked upright and reached for his bedside lamp all in one movement. In his panic he struck it with his arm and sent it flying. He heard the *pop* as the bulb shattered. He was hyperventilating and his heart was pounding in his ears, but all the same he thought he heard a sound somewhere in his room. Not the gentle mouse-like rustle he had heard before, but something closer to a footstep.

Fear washed over him like a waterfall. A part of him wanted to jump from the bed and make a dash for the door. Another, more primitive, part wanted to burrow under the bedclothes and hide. His body, acting of its own accord, compromised between the two and started to crawl down the length of the bed, still clutching the blanket.

Donny stopped. Now he moved, he could actually make out the picture on the faintly glowing poster. And it had changed again, more radically this time. Chuckie was no longer in the picture at all. And the cabin trunk was empty.

Donny recoiled. He was in the grip of such a terror now that he no longer trusted his eyes. He scrambled panic-stricken back along the bed away from the nightmare poster. He *knew* it couldn't have changed that much. Dammit, he knew it couldn't be on the wall. It was locked in the back of his cupboard and, even if Aileen had crept into his room, she didn't have the key. It had to be a trick of the light. It *had* to be!

He remembered the night light on his bedside table. He sometimes used it instead of the electric lamp. There were matches there too, somewhere. He needed light. He needed enough light in his room to see what was going on. He needed light more than he needed to breathe.

The sound like a footfall came again. Desperately Donny fumbled for the matches. There was a slight rattle of the box as something placed them firmly in his hand.

9

"I don't know if these bundles are worth it," Peter Flynn said sourly.

"'Course they are!" said Harry Foster. "What's 50p against the chance of getting something really cool?"

"This is my last one," Pete said. "There's *never* anything decent in them." He started to open the package at once with Harry standing right beside him. It was junk, just as he thought. "Definitely my last –"

He stopped. At the bottom of the package was a neatly rolled-up movie poster for the old horror flick *Child's Play*. It showed Chuckie the doll carrying a long knife and walking away from a cabin trunk which contained bits of a dismembered body and a severed human head.

"See?" said Harry. "Didn't I tell you you'd find something cool?"

The head was turned away, but from some reason it reminded Pete of Donny Beck, who'd gone missing back in the autumn. He looked across at Harry and smiled broadly. "Yeah, I have to hand it to you Harry – this one really is cool for a change."

A TERRIBLE MISTAKE

Maeve Friel

By the time a weak sun had risen over the island, small groups were already coming out of their wretched cabins and hurrying towards the pier. They were young people for the most part, mainly in their late teens, and you could sense their excitement in the way they walked down the stony paths across the bog, laughing and shouting and greeting their friends. By eight o'clock there were over a hundred of them standing on the pier, watching the hooker as it swung around the sound in full sail and anchored in the channel a few hundred yards offshore. A little flotilla of black currachs was already ferrying passengers out to the larger boat. The low blue line of hills, barely visible on the horizon, was the mainland twenty miles away.

Catherine Lavelle and her young brother, Thomas, were impatient to be off. They could hardly wait for their parents to say goodbye and let them go.

"Go on, Mother," said Catherine as her mother hugged her for the umpteenth time. "We'll be back before you know it."

"Look after Thomas, won't you? And Thomas, you look after your sister."

"We'll be all right. We'll write as soon as we're in Scotland."

"And send money as soon as we get our first pay," added Thomas.

"The currach is waiting for us, Mother. We must go."

"Come on, if you're coming. The tide is going out fast," shouted a man at the foot of the stone steps of the pier. "You'll miss the boat if you're not careful."

Catherine gave her mother one final kiss, grabbed her brother by the arm and ran down to the steps to board the last currach. As the oarsman took up his oars, she turned and waved. High above her on the pier, the families left behind waved back and shouted last-minute goodbyes and instructions which were carried off unheard into the wind.

Seán Scanlon, the skipper of the hooker, helped them clamber up over the side of the boat.

"That's a hundred and five passengers we have on board," said his brother, the currachman.

"No harm," said Seán. "Sure, I've had one hundred and twenty on before this. At sixpence each, I take it you're not complaining."

Catherine pushed her way through the crowd. By any standard, the boat was overcrowded. There was barely room to move. One of her father's friends, a man called Patrick Joyce, was sitting up on the gunwhales, dangling his legs over the side. He squeezed up to make room for Catherine and her brother to join him.

"It's a good sailing breeze," he said. "It should be a nice trip over to the port."

"The steamer wouldn't leave for Glasgow without us, would it?" asked Thomas.

"Not a bit of it," said Patrick. "Though some day soon,

when you're bent double in the dirt digging potatoes in a Scottish field with your back half broken and your fingers blue and stiff with the cold, you might wish it had."

"It's not that bad, is it, Patrick?"

"Bad enough," he replied. "Though maybe the first time's not the worst. It's knowing what lies ahead of you, year after year, that makes your heart sore. God knows it's a harsh world we live in when fourteen- and fifteen-year-olds like you have to leave their own country to pay the rates to our English landlords."

Catherine looked back at the island, disappearing now behind a swirl of clouds. All round her, her friends and neighbours chattered excitedly. Like her, most of the younger ones had never left home before and were looking forward to the journey to Scotland, and to seeing what life was like beyond the poor barren island where they had been brought up. She felt grown up at last, able to earn money for the first time, money that was badly needed at home to pay the landlord's rent. And if the work was tough, at least, at the end of the season, she and Thomas would each have fifteen pounds to give to her mother.

The hooker skimmed along over the waves. They passed outcrops of rock, sleek and black with seaweed, where pot-bellied puffins stared impassively back at them, their comical red bills stuffed with tiny fish so that they looked as if they had drooping silver moustaches. Gulls, following in the wake of the boat, wheeled and screamed overhead, and here and there seals bobbed up from underneath the waves and somersaulted.

"This is the most beautiful place on earth," thought Catherine.

It was just after noon as the hooker drew near to the harbour. On the opposite side of the boat to where

Catherine was sitting, there was a sudden commotion. People began to stand up and point.

"Look, that's it!" someone shouted. "The Glasgow steamer."

A great cheer went up. Everyone began to push and jostle to get their first view of the great ship that was to take them to Scotland. Most of them had never seen such a sight before in their lives. They crowded over to the rails, yelling at their companions to "come and see the steamer". Passengers began to come up from the hold. The people sitting around Catherine and Thomas slid off the gunwhales and elbowed their way across to the other side of the boat.

As they did so, a sudden squall caught the hooker. It began to list.

People screamed out in fear as the hooker, still in full sail, tilted alarmingly.

"Lower the mainsail," Patrick Joyce shouted, but the skipper and his brother did not seem to hear him. Seán Scanlon was already yelling at the youngsters to sit down, to back away from the rails. His brother was at the helm, trying to bring the boat around in a sharp turn. He did not lower the sail.

The hooker went down in an instant. As it rolled over, Thomas leapt into the rigging. He stretched out a hand to haul Catherine after him but other hands reached up to clutch him and he was dragged, screaming, into the water. Others were trapped beneath the deck. Many more, knocked unconscious by the mast, tumbled over the side. They never stood a chance.

The captain of the steamer was undoubtedly the hero of the hour. In less than five minutes he had the small boats launched from his own deck. The boatmen scooped up as many of the flailing bodies as they could fit in one go and rowed as fast as they dared to shore. Boatload after boatload of bodies were carried out of the sea and laid on the pier. The injured were quickly taken away to hospital. But the final toll was great: as night fell, thirty corpses were lying on the floor of the harbour-master's office.

Catherine opened her eyes. She could see rafters above her and smelled the familiar smells of turf smoke and the sea. She recognised the tow and slide of water as the waves slipped up and down the beach outside. Home, she thought, but at once knew it could not be home.

The roof was too high, the walls too far away. A high window let in a pale watery moonlight. Am I already in Scotland? she wondered. Is this the boarding-house? She could not remember how she had got there. She felt intensely cold, colder than she had ever been in her life. Her head throbbed. She tried to sit up but found she could not move. Her whole body felt heavy; her arms and legs seemed to be pinned to the ground beneath her. They would not obey the messages her brain was sending them.

Somewhere in the room, she heard low moaning sounds, short squeals like the noise of a frightened rabbit. There was another noise too, a tapping, as if someone was drumming out a faint rhythm with their fingertips. Slowly she managed to turn her head towards the sound.

A row of dark humped shapes lay on the ground to her left. She narrowed her eyes, recoiled with horror as she saw what they were. A line of bodies stretched away down the room. She could make out faces she knew. There, next to her, with his head turned towards her at a strange angle, was Patrick Joyce, her father's friend. There were tendrils of seaweed clinging to his hair.

Waves of fractured memories hurtled towards her. She

remembered the hooker suddenly listing, the bodies slipping and sliding towards the rails, the sound of wood snapping as the mast broke, the howls and shrieks as the ship suddenly capsized. Thomas flinging himself up into the rigging, stretching his hand out to take hers. Then nothing. A terrible silence had come down. She had been alone in the water, she remembered, bobbing like a cork float, for what seemed like hours. At last, arms had reached out towards her and she had felt herself being dragged over the side of the boat.

At least I am alive, she thought. And in hospital. She wondered if her mother had learned of the disaster yet, hoped that she knew that Catherine was alive. If only she knew Thomas was all right too.

The room was so silent she could hear her heart beating. It was bitterly cold. She tried again to reach down and pull a blanket around her but could not make her arms work. Something sticky and wet was dripping slowly across her forehead into her eyes. Her head throbbed worse than ever. Why did the nurses not come?

The drumming noise at the far end of the room had started up again. There were other noises too, coming from another direction, shufflings, scratchings. She hoped it was not a rat. Suddenly, one of the humped shapes near her reared up out of the darkness. A head turned in her direction, its wild eyes flying open, then fell back again out of sight. It was Seán Scanlon, the skipper. Catherine opened her mouth to scream but all that came out was a strangled croak.

The moon had moved in front of the window, casting long shadows against the wall. In the moonlight, Patrick Joyce's face was white and waxy. His head lolled to one side, like a doll with a broken neck.

"Patrick," she whispered. "Are you awake?"

There was no answer but, at the sound of her voice, the drumming at the other side of the room grew louder.

"Who's there?" she said. Her voice tore at her throat. No one answered her.

The chill coming up through the stone floor froze her to the bone. I will die of cold, she thought. What sort of people are they that have not even given us a blanket? Tears began to slowly run down her cheeks. She wanted to be at home, snug and safe in her own bed with her little sisters. Then it dawned on her. We are not in beds. Why have they not put us in beds? Why has no one come to fix Patrick's neck? She heard her own voice answer her. Because this is not a hospital. These people are all dead. And they think I am dead too.

Inch by painful inch, she managed to move her neck to look down the other side of the room. Another line of bodies stretched away from her. In the light of the moon, they were fallen ivory statues, their faces hard and drained of colour, their limbs stiff. There was Bridget Healy who had been at school with her. And Kit McFadden, who had played the fiddle at the farewell ceilí the night before. Dear God, she prayed, let someone come soon and find me before they bury me alive.

The moon had moved off out of sight. Through the high rectangle of the window, Catherine could just make out a pale grey sky with punched clouds. The wind whistled in the chimneybreast. The pain in her head was blinding. The sticky stuff around her eyes had hardened. It itched but she could not move her hand to rub at it.

The drumming at the far end of the room was growing fainter.

There was someone else there, someone like her who was not dead.

17

"Who is it?" she croaked. "This is Catherine Lavelle. Can you hear me? Tap twice if you can hear me."

The fingers tapped twice.

"Can you move?"

The fingers tapped once.

"Thank God I am not alone," she whispered to the tapping fingers. "It will be morning soon. Someone will come and get us then."

"Are you a boy or a girl?" Catherine asked. "Tap once for a girl."

The fingers tapped once, then after a long pause, tapped again. Whoever her companion was, he was very weak.

"Be brave," said Catherine. "Don't give up. It is almost light."

Her head felt so light, so dizzy. She began to drift in and out of sleep, lulled at first by sweet dreams of home, of running free on the far side of the island where there is no horizon but water, but the cold and the pain would not let her rest. She opened her eyes, disconcerted, not knowing where she was and wept bitterly to find herself still in that awful place with death closing in around her. Her heart-beat was so slow, she was afraid she might die there all alone.

"Are you still there? Answer me," she said, but the drumming fingers had fallen silent.

"God help me," she prayed, and with a great effort of will, she raised her hand to her throbbing forehead.

The day dawned bright and clear. As the clock in the church tower struck seven, Detective Inspector Cooney and the chairman of the local Board of Guardians made their way towards the harbour-master's store. The sea was as calm as a millpond. The Scottish steamer lay at anchor beside the quay and a row of three hookers was gliding up the channel. The only evidence of the awful tragedy of the day before were the pitiful belongings of the shipwrecked emigrants strewn along the strand. There was the bright scarlet red of a young girl's cloak, there a tweed hat or bonnet. The straw baskets which had carried their food for the journey bobbed about on the waves lapping against the harbour walls.

Outside the makeshift morgue, the relatives stood in silent grief, waiting to come in and identify their dead. As a procession of carts, each laden with a pile of plain wooden coffins, turned in to the quayside, the silence was broken by eerie high-pitched cries as the women began to keen.

Detective Inspector Cooney held up a hand to stop the crowd surging forward.

"Just a minute," he said softly.

The two men stepped inside the store and closed the wide double doors behind them.

"Merciful Jesus," said the chairman. "Will you look at that?"

Only feet in front of them, out of line from the other corpses, was the cold dead body of Thomas Lavelle. He had rolled over on to his stomach and lay with his hand stretched out in front of him, his fingers curled in a tight fist.

"He must have been alive when we left him," said the detective, crossing himself. "He must have been trying to crawl to the door."

"And look there! Another one!" said the other man.

In the middle of the front row of the drowned victims, was another body, young Catherine Lavelle, one white hand shielding her eyes from the cruel scenes to either side of her.

"We must say nothing, nothing," said the chairman. "Do you hear, man?" he repeated urgently. "Not a word. It was just a mistake, a terrible mistake. It would be more than the parents could bear to know that their poor children were abandoned here among the dead." The policeman nodded, his eyes filled with tears.

Together they carefully raised the poor lifeless body of Thomas and carried him back to lie beside the other corpses. They gently drew Catherine's arm down by her side and closed her eyes.

Outside, the keening grew louder. Detective Inspector Cooney walked unsteadily to the door and motioned to the coffin-bearers to come in and box up the dead. Catherine, still clinging to the last fragile thread of her life, felt the heat of the sunlight stream into the room. Then a dark shadow fell over her face as the coffin lid was lowered.

KNICK-KNOCK
Michael Carroll

It started as a bit of a joke, you know?

We thought it was a laugh. We thought that the old geezer would get pissed off with us, and that would be that.

You see, we were all fourteen or fifteen years old, and bored. Not the sort of bored you get in school or in church, but the sort of bored you can only get when you're too old to play with toys and too young and too broke to go anywhere.

It was a never-ending summer of rain and hailstones, and even the boredom of school looked attractive.

So one night, when we were hanging around the corner of the cul-de-sac with nothing to do – there weren't even any girls around that we could torment – Billy suggested that we go across the estate to the big old house, and see if there was anything happening there.

The others just shrugged, but I thought it was a good idea. "Yeah," I said, and poked Mark in the chest. "Remember when we were kids? You used to think that place was haunted."

Billy smirked. "Ah, leave the pansy alone, Mike. He'll wet his knickers."

I laughed. "Doesn't matter, he probably still wears plastic pants anyway."

Mark glared angrily at me, but said nothing. He was always like that. He only hung around with the three of us because he had nothing else to do. We didn't mind him hanging around because it was a good laugh picking on him. Besides, he was a bit of a wimp. You need someone like him in your gang, to act as a lookout when you're nicking stuff at the newsagent's. He was always too scared to steal anything himself, but he was too afraid of us not to do what he said.

Like Mark, Donal was also very quiet. Well, most of the time. He was bigger than the rest of us, and handy in case we got into a scrap. He was leaning against the lamppost and giving his nose a good pick. It was something else to watch him at work: he had his little finger right up there – all of his other fingers were too big – digging away furiously. He even kept the nails on his little fingers long so that he could have a really good pick.

So anyway, we started to head over to the old house. On the way, I pointed to a house and told Mark that my cousin lived there, and that he was to ring the bell and ask him to come with us. We waited by the gate, just behind the car. As soon as Mark pressed the doorbell, me and Billy jumped on the car's bonnet and set off the alarm, then the three of us ran for it.

Mark was out of breath and swearing madly at us by the time he caught up. At least, he was swearing as madly as he could – Mark was one of those people who felt uncomfortable using real swear-words. He told us we were a pack of bloody eejits and a bunch of dirty scabs. He stopped short of calling us a load of meanies like he did once: we'd had such a laugh at that, because his second name is Meany.

We'd made the usual jokes about his father having put himself about a bit when he was younger.

I was starving, so we stopped at the chipper on the way, but the sour git who runs the place wouldn't let us in, because we called him names the last time. I tried to make Mark go in and get the stuff, but after the trick we'd already played on him, he told me to go to hell.

After about half an hour, we reached the big house. We stood at the gate, looking down the long driveway. The house was well over a hundred years old, one of those big old buildings made out of faded red bricks and covered in more drainpipes than ivy.

By that time it was pretty dark, and it suddenly occurred to me that I'd never seen the house at night before. It looked a lot different. In the daylight, the house seemed like a more or less random collection of old bricks, it looked as though the whole place would collapse if someone slammed the front door.

But in the darkness, it was solid. I had the strangest feeling that the house had been there forever, and would still be there long after everything else was gone.

I realised then that Billy was talking to me. "What was that?" I asked, turning to him.

Billy pointed towards the house. "I said someone's living there. Look."

He was right. There was a light on in one of the downstairs windows, and we could see someone moving around.

"Bummer," I said. "I thought the place was abandoned."

Mark looked relieved. "Well, that's that. Let's go home." He started to walk away, but Donal reached out and grabbed him by the arm.

"Where're you goin', ya bleedin' girl?" Donal asked.

"I'm just going home. It's getting late."

Billy laughed. "Yeah! His mammy'll have put out his pyjamas already."

"Not the ones with the bunnies?" I asked.

"Nah, I think he's got the Disney ones tonight."

Mark shook off Donal's arm. "Ah, give it a rest, you lot."

Billy put his arm around Mark's shoulders and said, "Listen, if you want to prove that you're a real man, and not a girl, I have a little test for you."

Mark raised his eyes. "For crying out loud, not another bloody test!"

Billy shoved Mark through the gateway. "Ring yer man's doorbell and run away. You've already had a bit of practice tonight."

Mark looked at the house for a few seconds, then turned around and tried to push past us. I locked my arm around his neck, and forced him to the ground.

As usual, he didn't even put up a fight; he just said, "Okay! Okay! I'll do it."

I let him up, then gave him another push in the direction of the house.

As slowly as he could, Mark trudged towards the house. He did his best to be quiet on the gravel path, but even a deaf man would have heard him. It didn't occur to the fool to walk on the grass.

Eventually, he got to the porch. It was pretty dark, and we couldn't see him too well, but we heard the knocker pounding on the door. Then Mark was charging back up the driveway, his arms and legs going all over the place like he was trying to scare pigeons or something.

The rest of us were laughing too hard to stop him as he ran past us and kept going. We barely even made it behind the hedge before the old man came out and stood in the doorway looking around. Through the gaps in the hedge we could see him scratching his head.

Billy was laughing so loudly he almost gave us away. I slapped my hand over his mouth to shut him up, but he started snorting instead, so I pinched his nose closed.

After a few minutes, the old man stepped back into the house and closed the door. Billy pushed my hands away. "Jesus! You nearly suffocated me, Mike!"

I said nothing. I just looked at Donal, who was still sniggering. "So who's next, Donal? You?"

Donal – who wasn't one of the world's great thinkers – considered this for a few seconds. "Yeah. It'll be a laugh."

Billy rubbed his neck, and swore at me. "You nearly suffocated me!"

"Yeah, yeah," I said. "Stop whinging, you moaner."

We gave the old man another few minutes to settle down, then Donal lumbered his way down the drive. Even though he was probably twice Mark's weight, he was a lot quieter . . . and he was a lot faster running back.

This time, the old man was really annoyed, which was even funnier. I thought that he'd hear us sniggering and march across the garden towards us, but he just stood there in the doorway, glaring.

He took a full ten minutes to close the door, and by that time we were getting cold and stiff from kneeling in the one position.

Donal stood up and rubbed his massive hands together, to get some life back into them. "I'm goin' home," he announced. "It's shaggin' freezin' out here."

"Me too," Billy said, getting to his feet. His voice was a little rough, I noticed. Maybe I'd held his mouth and nose closed for a bit too long. He was staring at me with hurt in his eyes, and I knew that he'd probably try to beat the crap out of me next chance he had.

Donal looked at me. "Comin'?"

I shrugged. "Nah. I'm going to have a go myself." I don't know why I said that. What is the point of knocking on someone's door and running away if there's no one around to watch?

Billy and Donal turned and walked away. I could hear that they were talking, and I was pretty sure that Billy was telling Donal that I'd done something bad on him, just so that Donal would be on his side if it came to a fight.

I stood up and stamped my feet a bit, to try and get some life back into them. I looked towards the house, and saw that the light was still on downstairs.

I should have just walked away. I mean, there's no point in doing a knick-knock on your own.

But I walked down the drive anyway. I was careful not to walk on the gravel, so that my approach was as quiet as possible. I reached the porch, and grabbed the huge doorknocker.

The instant the knocker hit the door, the door opened and the old man was standing there, right in front of me. He was wearing his shirt open to the third button, and I noticed that he had a thick dark scar around his throat, showing clearly against his white skin. In fact, his whole body was a mass of scars: his hands, his arms, his chest and face. He was a big guy, too. He looked as though he'd once been a boxer or something.

I was so shocked I didn't even run.

The old man grinned, then pushed the door open wider. "Come on in, you must be freezing."

I stared at him. "What?"

"You *are* the lad who's come to collect the paintings,

aren't you? They said you'd be here at six." He looked at his watch. "Well, you're nearly five hours late. I can't give you the full fifty pounds."

My mind went into overdrive. Fifty pounds, or close enough to it . . . plus whatever these paintings were worth. I did my best to look apologetic. "Sorry I'm late." I gestured towards the driveway. "As you can see, I don't have the van with me. I had a puncture. I would have phoned to let you know, but they didn't give me your number."

The old man nodded. "That's because I don't have a phone." He gestured for me to follow him inside. "Well, it's very good of you to come by to let me know."

As I passed through the doorway, I suddenly felt a lot warmer. "Wow! I didn't realise how cold it was outside until I came in."

He nodded. "Are you hungry? Thirsty?"

I was about to say that I was starving, but suddenly I didn't feel hungry anymore. "No . . . not at all."

Then the old man started to laugh. "Good. Good." He suddenly reached out and locked his huge scarred hand around my throat, then slammed me back against the wall.

He curled his left hand into a fist and shook it threateningly. I could see the dirty, ragged nails cutting into his palms. "Do you know how long I've been here, boy? *Do you know how long?*"

I shook my head as well as I could. "No, sir," I said, trying to swallow. "I'm sorry about the lads knocking on your door. I only came to apologise."

He leaned closer, and hissed into my face. *"Liar!"* His breath stank of rotting flesh and foul water. His dry, cracked lips peeled back to reveal rotten, yellowing teeth.

Then he started to laugh again. He released his hand and I dropped gasping to the floor.

He stared down at me. "He told me someone would come. He told me that someone would come to the door."

I tried to stand up, but he kicked my legs from under me. "You stay there, boy, and listen while I tell you the rules."

I stared up at him, trying to ignore the pain in my throat and ankles. "What do you mean?"

"I'll tell you what I mean . . ." He crouched down, and hissed into my face again. "I'm going to walk out that door, and leave this place. You will stay here." He snorted. "I've done my time. Now you do yours."

He slapped me across the face. "You think you're so damned clever, don't you?" He slapped me again, this time with the other hand. "You think you're a big man." Another slap. "You're nothing, boy. You're less than nothing."

He stood up, and looked at the door. He was silent for a long time, then with a calm, clear voice he said, "I have been in this house for over one hundred and sixty *years*." He turned to me again, and spat right into my open mouth.

I suddenly felt as though my stomach was on fire. I lurched forward and my muscles spasmed; I heaved what was left in my stomach on to the wooden floor.

"It's your turn, boy. I was like you, you know. Thought I was a big man. Pushed my friends around, treated everyone like dirt." He reached out and touched the door. "I made the same mistake that you did. I thought it would be fun to knock on this door and run away.

"The man who caught me told me the rules . . . you will remain here, ageing very slowly, not eating, not sleeping, unable to leave the house, unable to do anything but wait."

I rolled over on to my back, not caring that I was lying in a pool of my own vomit. "Wait for what?" I asked, gasping for breath.

"Wait for your rescuer. Wait for the young man to take you place." He grinned once more. "You cannot leave until he arrives. He will knock at the door."

I nodded. "I understand."

"No, I don't think you do. Not yet. You see, your rescuer will only come once. If you fail to answer the door to him, he will be gone and you will stay here forever."

Again, I nodded. I couldn't understand what point the old man was trying to make, but I didn't want to say anything.

He looked at me once more, then opened the door. "At last, I can leave. At last I can die."

Without looking back, the old man stepped out into the night. He paused for a few seconds, then walked away, laughing madly.

I got to my feet slowly, and tried to follow him, but somehow I couldn't get past the door.

I was still too shocked by everything to realise that what he said was true. Unable to leave, I wandered around the house, but it was only as I started to go upstairs that I finally understood everything that he'd said to me.

Tied to the banister rail above the stairs was an old length of rope. I remembered the vivid scar around the old man's throat, and the scars all over his hands and chest, and I knew than that this was hell.

I've been here a long time now.

And every time I hear a knock, I go out into the hall and open the door.

There's never anyone there.

But there will be. One day.

THE BEAST
Ivy Bannister

He might have chosen any of the others. Jenny, for example, who lived in the house on the hill, and whose father ran the golf club. Or Katherine, whose beautiful face was framed by a cloud of red hair. They were all mad for him.

"Honor O'Neill," her mother said, "you're only fourteen years of age. You've got to be sensible. There's something odd about a fella who has nothing better to do than hang around the school gate, chatting up the girls."

"Mmm," Honor said.

"Besides," he mother sniffed, "he looks foreign."

He did, too. It was part of his charm. His complexion was sallow, his hair was dark, and he looked like he shaved every day. Although he was by no means tall, he had fleshed out like an adult, and there was a wolfish, but exciting look to his eyes.

"I'd watch out for that one, if I were you," Honor's mother said. "Even his name is peculiar. Who ever heard of calling their son Morgan?"

Morgan. It was an interesting name, that suggested

something out of the ordinary. The girls were inclined to repeat it, unnecessarily, just because they liked the sound of it. Yes, they were all fascinated by him, so Honor paid no heed to her mum, and listened with the others whenever she could to the young man's far-fetched tales of distant places.

And when, in the end, he asked her to run away with him, Honor was both flattered and excited. "We'll be going to the very edge of the universe," he said.

Honor laughed. She didn't believe him, no more than she'd believed her mother's warning. Without stopping to think, Honor stuffed a few things into a canvas hold-all – a mirror, some underthings, an extra jumper – just what she could carry. Then, recklessly, she turned her back on the world that she knew.

It was a difficult journey. The planes that they took first were not uncomfortable, but the flights were long. They seemed to criss-cross the earth in what appeared to be a southerly direction. After the aeroplanes, things got harder. The draughty steam train rattled her bones; and the people around them peered at her with hard hostile faces.

"What's the matter with them?" Honor whispered. "Why are they staring?"

"Because that's the way they are," Morgan answered. Nonetheless he spoke to them sharply in their guttural tongue, until they looked away.

How was it that Morgan knew their language? Suddenly Honor was afraid to ask. Too late, she'd realised how little she knew about her companion.

At least, when they got to the desert, they were alone again. The nights were so cold that her teeth ached. The days were worse. Sometimes, when the hot wind scoured sand into her eyes, she wondered how she could go on. But she didn't complain. Not to Morgan. Instead she looked at his silent, stocky body ploughing on ahead, and she wondered. What if she fell down? Would he look back? Would he notice? Or would he simple leave her flesh to rot on the sand until the sun bleached her bones?

At the edge of the desert, she began to feel better. A blush of green broke through the white sands, and the air was pleasant. Then Honor felt satisfied, satisfied with herself for forging the new reserves of energy that had got her there safely.

Morgan was pleased too. He offered her the gun. "Would you like a shot?" He gestured ahead at a herd of antelope that was grazing in the distance.

Honor took the gun without flinching, although its stock was heavy with silver filigree. She sensed that it was a compliment to be asked, but also a test that she could not fail. She examined the weapon. Its double barrel flared like a bull's nostrils in the sunlight. Only a few weeks back, she would have been terrified even to hold such a thing, much less point it at an animal. Now she gritted her teeth and hoisted it high, its butt against her shoulder. She fired. Once, and then once again, absorbing the kick in her shoulder. In the distance, an antelope dropped like a stone.

He laughed, a deep, throaty laugh, and tossed her hat into the air. "I like you because you're different!" he shouted, baring his teeth. "None of the others have survived! I like you because you have no fear!"

Her heart quickened. His admiration washed over her, making her glow with pride and with happiness. But somewhere, deep inside, a warning voice niggled. "'None of the others have survived.'" What did that mean? Had he taken this journey before? Had there been others? And if so, what had become of them?

So, even though she wanted to fling her arms around Morgan, and to tell him that she liked him too, she didn't. She bit her tongue and said nothing.

Instead, she did something she had only read about in books. She disembowelled the antelope, plunging her knife into its still warm underbelly, spilling out the soft yellows and purples of its entrails. The antelope's blood seeped into the sand, binding the white grains into crimson clots. The sight sickened Honor a little, but she felt bound to Morgan by bands of invisible steel, and that she must do whatever he wanted.

She realised that she must love him. How else could he exert such control over her? But perhaps it was then, as she studied the dead animal on the sand, that she began to hate Morgan too.

They wandered on. The sands receded, and monkeys screeched overhead. The bush closed in around them. They were in the jungle. Morgan led them along faint tracks that wound through the undergrowth. They ate meat from the antelope and fruit from the trees. "We need water," he said, as Honor followed him into a native village.

Inquisitive and shrill, the village girls crowded about her, jostling her, the naked expanses of their ebony flesh as shiny as ice in the burning sun. Honor envied them the freedom to live in their skins. Chattering wildly, they nudged her away from Morgan.

She realised how mysterious she must appear to them, with the many layers of clothing she wore to protect her from the sun and insects. Curiously, their dark fingers investigated, creeping under her hat and petticoats, up the soiled sleeves of her jacket and down her collar. Did she

33

have hair, as they did? Did she have arms and legs, this queer, white-faced creature in their midst?

Across the way, Morgan was not submitted to such indignities. The villagers, who seemed to know him, had gathered round. A man, whom Honor judged to be chieftain on the basis of his elaborate headdress, was speaking in tones of bitter complaint, as he gesticulated towards the jungle. The women howled in agreement. Morgan listened, stroking the beard that he'd grown since their flight. His hair had grown too, Honor thought, long and thick, making him look more like a wolf than ever.

Shaking off the village girls, Honor crossed over. "What is it?" she asked. "What are they talking about?"

"Some sort of a beast, apparently. It's been on the rampage in these parts."

The chieftain crashed his hands together, angry words flooding from his lips.

"He says it breathes fire," Morgan said. "He says it's tall, taller than a man. It's got the head of a lion, and wings, and the body of a horse. He says it's more dangerous than an army of two thousand."

The villagers trembled and groaned.

"I'd like to see this beast," Morgan said, his eyes flashing with excitement.

He spoke to the villagers in a voice that was brusque and commanding. They listened, sometimes rolling their eyes, other times clicking their tongues. Eventually the man with the headdress fell on to his knees before Morgan, touching his fingers to the tips of Morgan's boots.

"Why is he doing that?" Honor asked.

"Because I have agreed to kill the beast."

They left the village together with the chieftain, whose name was Frangandi, and thirty native men: bearers, hunters and pathfinders. After a while, Morgan fell back, letting the men press ahead through the bush. Honor paced her step to Morgan's, exactly as he expected. When he stopped, she stopped too, allowing him to push her against the gnarled trunk of an ancient banyan tree. Pinioning her arms against the wood, he kissed her. She closed her eyes and kissed him back. The spongy bark from the tree crumbled against her shoulders.

Kissing Morgan was different from kissing the other boys she had known. It was like a drug that made her forget her doubts, that made her glad that she'd run away. It even helped convince her that his plan to kill the beast was both sensible and desirable.

When Honor opened her eyes again, she saw something move in the foliage.

"Someone is watching us," she said softly.

Morgan laughed carelessly. "It's only him. Frangandi. You would expect him to watch. He won't take his eyes off me until I've kept my promise."

And so they tracked the beast, pursuing it by day and resting at night. They penetrated the darkest parts of the jungle, where no humans had travelled before, the pathfinders hacking out new ways through the undergrowth with their gleaming machetes.

Sometimes at night, they could hear the beast, its roar so loud that the earth itself shuddered, and the sooty smell from its breath hung over them like a malignant cloud. Then the native men were openly terrified. It was only Frangandi's more immediate threats that stopped them from bolting back the way they had come. And even Morgan looked white, beneath his hairy face and sallow skin.

Only Honor remained calm, for she detected something

else in that roar. What was it? she wondered. A mournful note? A sadness that such a beast should be hunted like a common animal?

As weeks passed into months, they drew closer. One night, after camp was pitched, Morgan said, "This is it. The beast is close. It has taken refuge beneath the cliff. It can go no further. We will shoot the beast tomorrow."

Honor slept poorly that evening, tossing and turning in her tent, disturbed by vivid dreams of violence and death.

In the morning, she rooted in her filthy hold-all for her mirror. It was the only thing that she still possessed from her former life, and it looked old. The silver backing was flaking away from the glass, and she could barely make out her own reflection. She looked old in the mirror, unnaturally old for her fourteen years. Could it be – could it possibly be? – that only six months had passed since she'd run away from home?

She ran her fingers over her face, tracing her cheekbones, the slender ridge of her nose and the bony jut of her jaw. Her eyes had a yellowish tinge and her lips were caked with dust. She slung the mirror back into the hold-all, hardly caring if it shattered, because she didn't want to look at the stranger she'd become.

She closed her eyes and allowed herself to think, longingly, of home. She pictured her bed with its soft duvet. It was quite extraordinary to remember that there were places where people actually lived in houses with TVs and phones and microwaves. Honor yearned to go back. She wanted to be a schoolgirl once again. Images of her mother and father, and of her little brother, crept into Honor's head. Her whole body ached with the desire to walk into a familiar room, to hear English spoken again, to talk to somebody apart from Morgan.

But he would never allow her to go back. Honor knew it, so she squared her shoulders and put the past out of her mind.

She set about the difficult business of washing herself. The tin basin held only a few inches of water. But her whole body itched with grime. Taking a precious scrap of coarse brown soap, she raised a small lather and spread it carefully over her body. Then a bit at a time, she wiped the lather away with a rag, which she rinsed now and again in the water.

She pinched her cheeks to give them a bit of colour. All her make-up was long since gone; but still, instinctively, she set about looking her best for him.

Honor heard the insect before she saw it, a bright whirr of green descending towards her still wet arm. For a moment she watched it plant its prickly legs on her skin. It wriggled its metallic abdomen, then bit. Only then did she slap, spattering its greenness, but it was too late. The insect's jaw remained locked in her flesh. She pinched it out with her fingernails. A drop of her own blood glittered on her forearm, vivid against the white of her skin.

She flicked the remains of the insect on to the dirt. Outside her tent, the natives were moving around the clearing. They grunted and swore in their incomprehensible language. The fire hissed. She could smell meat cooking for their breakfast. Antelope meat. Suddenly, her memory of the antelope that she'd shot, and of its startled eyes frozen in death, filled her head. She shuddered. No, she would not eat antelope this time; she would not touch it even if she starved. But at least she had learned how to use the gun.

Morgan was going to shoot the beast. Was it possible, she wondered, that she, Honor O'Neill, didn't want him to?

There were red welts rising on Honor's arm from the

bite. She studied them with interest. They didn't hurt. She felt only a faint throbbing beneath her skin. And the shape of the welts was clear: two perfect half moons with a spiral coiling between them. They were like hieroglyphs, the ancient Egyptian picture-writing that she remembered from school.

She heard the bark of his voice through the tent wall. He wanted her. For the moment, she forgot how unhappy she was. She felt herself turn towards him, like a magnetised needle pulled towards the north.

Feverishly, she dressed. The dead insect glittered underfoot. She picked it up and slipped it between her lips, crushing it with her tongue until its metallic taste coated her mouth. Then she stepped out into the light.

Morgan was loading the gun. "A careful huntsman looks after his own shot," he said. She looked at the shiny bullets, the instruments of death. He rammed them deep into the double-barrel. The welts on her arm tingled.

The villagers had smeared their faces with clay and feathers. Frangandi took his drum. He played, softly at first, rhythmically tapping with cupped palms. The natives began to sway, punctuating the rhythm with soft grunts. Bit by bit, the pace quickened. Soon the clearing boiled with raging natives, their painted bodies caught up in a frenzied dance. Then, at a cry from Morgan, they seized their spears and machetes and vanished, fanning out into the green towards the cliff.

Morgan thrust the heavy gun into Honor's hands. "Carry," he barked. She took it, plunging after him into the undergrowth. Almost at once they were in a dark gloom under the thick roof of leaves. Masses of timber reared up around them, ancient cedars and huge pandanus trees, their black limbs heavy with ropes of twisting creeper.

Keeping her eyes fixed on Morgan's back, she paced him, stretching each step so as to place her feet in the indentations made by his own. A strange drugging peace settled upon her, as if nothing mattered but him and her and the moment, in that strange remote place. She watched him bend to the beast's tracks, the sweat gleaming on the back of his thick neck. He picked up earth, kneaded it between his fingers and sniffed.

On and on, she followed. She sensed the cliff was near. Slowly the foliage thinned. Patches of blue splashed down from above. The leaves paled from black to emerald, bathed in the gilt of the sun. Suddenly she saw the rock face, soaring above them.

Morgan smacked his lips. "Over there," he muttered. "That thicket there. Beware. The beast will crouch and spring." Without turning, he held back his hand for the gun, the gun he expected her to give him. She saw the curling hairs on the back of his hand, and the rough ovals of his fingernails.

Suddenly, a strange bellow filled the air, a throaty, shuddering trumpet that filled her with excitement. He tensed.

"Morgan!" she called. His name fluted out from between her lips like a silver arrow.

Pivoting, he turned sharply. He had only a moment, just enough time to see her sling the gun, with one sure movement, up to her shoulder. She fired. Once, then once again. His wolfish head split open like a ripe plum.

From somewhere in the green, Frangandi's eyes darted, red like a serpent's among the fronds. She knew he was watching, and she was pleased. She dropped the gun. Holding her head high, she glided ahead, striding alone and unarmed towards the thicket.

The villagers waited in an impassive semi-circle. When, at last, Honor emerged from the thicket leading the beast quietly on a hempen rope, they gasped. Her hands reached up to scratch its neck, paddling in its russet fur. It nuzzled her back with a smoky purr.

Delicately, she stretched out one of the beast's wings, tracing the translucent pinions and pearly webbing with her finger. For the beast was a very beautiful creature indeed, and she wanted the natives to admire it.

They prostrated themselves in wonder before girl and beast. She pushed up her sleeve, displaying her forearm. It was now marked clearly. A striking talisman rose from her flesh, two half moons and a spiral, metallic green in colour.

Honor smiled. She had travelled to the edge of the universe, but she had triumphed. Now she could go home again, back to her mother and father, and to her little brother, back to the life she missed so much. She could do it on her own. Nothing would stop her now.

Sun Day

Michael Scott

For a moment he thought his heart was going to burst. He could feel it pumping so hard against his chest that his skin was visibly trembling, and the veins in his forehead and neck had swelled so that they were physically uncomfortable.

"One last try," Declan Costello whispered. He rammed the iron prise bar deep into the hard earth beneath the stone, and threw his entire weight upon it.

The stone shifted, groaned and shifted again.

"Yes!" he breathed, leaning on the prise bar again. He knew he could do it; all it required was an iron prise bar, some sweat and a lot of determination.

Desperation would be more like it, he thought wryly; and God knows, but he was desperate enough.

The prize was the latest gimmick thought up by the presenter of one of the popular morning radio programmes. A bar of gold – with a value of just over twenty-five thousand pounds – had been hidden somewhere in Ireland, and each morning over a series of weeks, cryptic clues were given to the bar's whereabouts. Whoever found the bar of gold would get to keep it, or its value in cash.

The first few clues were simple, and in the beginning gold fever had swept the country, but it had gradually tapered off as the clues became harder and harder, impossible to interpret. However, as the weeks wore on and no one found the gold, the radio presenter began giving hints to the bar's whereabouts, and explaining the more difficult clues. The flagging interest was revived, and small ads began to appear in the newspapers as people offered to pool their knowledge and information and share the prize.

It was only a matter of time, Declan knew, before someone would put all the clues together and the prize would be lost.

Unless he was right.

And if he was . . . well, twenty-five thousand would sort out his problems with the moneylender, sort out the bank, pay off the mortgage. He shook his head quickly; how had he ever got into this mess?

"Greed and stupidity," he said aloud, his voice flat on the early morning air.

And it wasn't entirely his fault; Sara had played her part too, pushing, pushing, always pushing, nagging at him when one neighbour added an extension to their bungalow, and another went on holiday to the Canaries, or when a third put in a new kitchen.

But they simply never had enough left over to put by to save for luxuries. Childhood sweethearts, they had married at eighteen, laughingly dismissing their lack of money, saying they would live on love. But that was two years ago. It had never bothered Declan before, but now, when he saw his friends and neighbours with their small – and not so small – luxuries, he felt the first sting of jealousy.

And finally, when the man across the road – a small, insignificant, pot-bellied, bald grocer – bought an electric mower for his lawn, Declan finally snapped. The sight of the shiny machine was the last straw, as he struggled to mow his own grass with the same old rusty push-mower he had used for years. There was no extra money for an electric mower. There was no extra money at all, as his wife frequently reminded him . . .

However, while he had always been able to ignore her nagging, he could not ignore the soft, grumbling purr of the machine across the road. The very sound seemed to mock him. So he had gone to a moneylender – without telling Sara – and borrowed a few pounds to purchase a small electric lawnmower.

Sara had been incredulous. "When I think of all the things we need around this house!" she cried, her hands on her hips, lips drawn into a thin white line, as she watched him assemble it. "A new washing-machine, for example, and a . . . "

The list was very long. His purchase of the mower had given her the thin edge of the wedge to drive under his skin, and at last he was forced to buy the new washing-machine . . . and the fridge, the tumble-drier, the microwave . . .

It meant more trips to the moneylender, the interest mounting at a terrifying rate.

And then, when he had slipped behind on the payments, came the veiled – and not so veiled – threats, the sudden visits of large men to his home, reminding him that his interest was overdue, the late-night phone calls.

Declan Costello simply had to find the hidden gold bar.

He studied the clues assiduously, repeating them over and over, spending hours in the library going through the encyclopaedias, the dictionaries, the thesaurus, working out the answers. When he had worked out his answer, he thought, at first, that it was nothing but wishful thinking. However, when he checked the answer, he realised that he had been right the first time – everything pointed to the gold being hidden within a mile of his own house. If he was right – and he was, he knew he was – then the gold was buried beneath a tumble of stones on the crest of a hill just beyond the last row of bungalows sprawling out from the town. The hill was windswept and barren, its stark outline against the sky relieved only by a tangle of thorn trees and a straggle of gorse. The gorse was studded with golden blooms, however, and when the wind was right their sweetness drifted down to the bungalows, though no one paused to sniff the wind and enjoy them.

Declan Costello certainly had no time for appreciating nature's wild perfumes. The gold was there!

It had to be.

Had to be.

He was determined not to waste a moment . . . why, even now, someone was probably making their way to the hilltop in search of the gold – his gold. He was going to look for it today, even if it was a Sunday.

The wife had moaned at him, but she often moaned at him for not going to Mass.

"You go enough for both of us," he had growled at her as he gathered his tools.

She stood at the door of the shed and watched him. "Where are you going, then? And why do you need a shovel and a prise bar? What are you up to, Declan?"

He had shrugged. He didn't want to tell her just yet – if he was wrong, she'd never let him forget it. "You're always giving out to me about the garden," he smiled slyly. "I thought I'd go . . . uh . . . dig up some heather if I can find some, and put it in the rockery."

Sara Costello stared at her husband, nonplussed. In the two years of their marriage, he had only ever worked in the garden once . . . and been stricken with sunstroke. Unsure what to say, she finally muttered, "Well, that's good ... white heather would be nice, I think. It's good luck."

Good luck. Declan smiled inwardly. Good luck was what you made for yourself. God helped those who helped themselves.

With the shovel on his shoulder, he walked down the road to the hill. If his calculations based on the radio hints were right, the gold was under the largest stone in the tumbled pile. During spring, some fellow from the university had been up on this hill, measuring and photographing. Declan had later heard him interviewed on the local radio. The professor had claimed the stone was some sort of ritualistic marker.

"This place was probably where the Lughnasa celebrations for this area were held. In pagan times, the people used to gather on hilltops to offer the fruits of the harvest to the sun in thanksgiving. The first of August was one of the four great festival days of the pagan Celtic year."

Sweating on the hilltop, in the blistering noonday sun, Declan heard those words again and smiled to himself. Today was not only Sunday, it was the first of August. Lughnasa. An important pagan festival, if you believed in such things. He didn't.

Grunting, digging, moving stones, Declan paid attention to nothing but the task in hand.

He did not noticed when the sun went behind a cloud and shadows began to gather.

"You should not disturb sites like this," the folklorist from the university had said.

The old people, the local people who lived here when

all this was farmland, had probably said the same things, once. And they had probably used it as an excuse for not digging up the fields. But they were gone, washed away on the rising tide of modern and identical bungalows blighting the ancient landscape.

Declan continued digging. He had moved the mass of rocks surrounding the largest stone, inserted the bar beneath it, and was now gently levering it up. As he drew it free of the earth he shoved stones under it with his foot to keep it propped high enough so that he could feel under it with his hand.

The gold was here – it had to be here.

Part of his mind – cold and calmly rational – noted that the stone gave no sign of having been recently disturbed. Surely if the radio programme had buried their gold bar under there, there would be some indication? But maybe not; God knows how long it had been buried.

Declan went on working, oblivious to the growing darkness of the day.

"The sun was sacred to ancient farmers. We can be sure they went to great lengths to satisfy it. Perhaps they even offered sacrifices at places such as this. Perhaps the largest of these stones was a sacrificial altar long before the coming of St Patrick to Ireland.

"Even after the arrival of Christianity, the old traditions survived for centuries, almost to the present day.

"Until very recent time, games would have been held up here, races, dancing. Perhaps fires lit. Flowers laid in tribute at the summit of the hill. In Christian times this was called Fraochain Sunday in honour of the whortleberries ripening, and they would have been picked and offered in honour of the old ways."

Those half-forgotten words echoed in Declan Costello's mind as he got down on hands and knees and stretched a careful arm under the edge of the large stone, feeling for some roughness in the earth to indicate it had been dug recently.

Nothing.

Squinting in concentration, he lay down full length and stretched his arm farther.

There had to be . . . had to be.

His fingers touched something.

Cold.

Something . . . cold and smooth and hard.

Declan grunted in satisfaction. He tried again, but his questing fingers just about brushed the side of the object. His arm was not long enough. He would have to crawl further under the stone, and that meant lifting it higher.

He went back to work.

Around him, the shadows shifted. An observer standing off to one side might have thought they took the near-transparent forms of dancing people. Some appeared to be carrying baskets heaped with flowers and fruit as they neared the summit where Declan worked feverishly amid the tumble of rocks.

But there was no one to observe the shadows.

The sky grew darker still, and a cold wind sprang up.

"The ultimate purpose of all these celebrations, these rituals, was the same: they were designed to invoke the sun. Christian or pagan, the Irish have always adored the sun and longed for it to come and stay, to warm their flesh and grow their crops. No people love the sun more than we do, and sites like this have ancient connections of great power. It was as if that overpowering desire for sunshine was concentrated here, permeating the landscape."

Declan had the stone high enough now. He could crawl under it.

But before he did, he peered into an utter blackness one last time to make certain he was not deceiving himself, that the risk was worth the reward.

And it was.

A pinprick of cold yellow.

The gold was there.

He could see it clearly now, golden and glowing, far back under the stone! They must have set the gold bar right down on the bare earth and then lowered the stone back in place over it.

Without any further hesitation, he lay flat on the ground and wriggled under the tilted stone.

Behind him, the shadows closed in, twisting, shifting, twirling in the patterns of a ritual as old as the land, forming two lines facing one another, like an avenue, leading toward the pile of stones.

A soft chanting began, so soft that Declan Costello, grunting and wheezing as he forced himself farther underneath the stone, chin scraping the bare earth, hair brushing the top of the stone, did not hear it. Nor did he smell the sweet fragrance of ripe whortleberries.

But it was there.

Declan was only conscious of the golden gleam ahead of him. He reached out for it again, certain he could close his fist on it now and claim the gold bar that would change his life.

The chanting grew louder.

Now!

As his hand reached for the bar, Declan yelped in sudden dismay. Something hot had burned him!

He snatched back his hand, feeling the skin start to puff and blister. Above the moist dampness of the earth, he could smell the tang of burnt meat. The thing which he had taken to be a bar of gold was blazing hot now, shedding an increasing light that shone into his face and blinded him. The light intensified, heat exploded from it like a sunburst as the chanting beyond the stone rose audibly. The flesh on his face tightened across his cheekbones, his eyelashes and sparse hair curling, crisping.

Declan tried to wriggle backward and escape the flaming fury he had unearthed beneath the stone, the miniature sun roasting his eyeballs.

But it was too late.

The sun blazed on . . .

. . . and ghostly hands tugged, ghostly shoulders pushed, and the great stone fell back into place, crushing him beneath its ageless weight . . .

. . . completing the Sun-day sacrifice.

THE LAND OF MY DREAMS

Eileen Dunlop

The smell hit Jack the moment he opened the door of his bedroom in his parents' new flat. He knew what it was; he'd smelt it every time he'd visited Gran in the geriatric hospital before she died. Disinfectant, masking more embarrassing smells. The odd thing was that Mum didn't seem to notice. Beaming from ear to ear she leapt around opening drawers and cupboards, proudly telling Jack what everything in the room had cost.

"Isn't it wonderful, Jack? Just imagine us living in a place like this!"

Jack was opening his mouth to point out that the place stank, but then shut it again. He'd just arrived, and it made sense to delay the wiping out of Mum's smile. She had a thing about smells and she wasn't a reasonable woman.

So he said, "Brilliant," then tried holding his breath.

"I'll leave you to settle in, dear," said Mum, smoothing the already immaculate duvet cover. "Lunch in the kitchen today. I'm getting the dining-room ready for the house-warming tomorrow evening."

Jack didn't reply. He could hardly wait for Mum to shut the door before throwing up the window sash and leaning out over the sill. Thankfully he took gulps of warm June air and sniffed the scent of newly-cut grass.

Looking across acres of lawn and colourful flower-beds, Jack knew exactly why Mum thought she was in heaven. She'd always yearned to live somewhere posher than a semi-detached in Rutherglen, and the opportunity to move to "an elegant apartment in Rattray House, former home of Glasgow shipping magnates" had come at just the right time for her. The semi-detached and Gran's flat had been sold, Dad's redundancy lump sum commandeered, and here she was in the land of her dreams.

"Such a coincidence, us having the same name as the shipping family!" she had chirruped down the 'phone to Jack, who was on a modern language course in London. "And imagine, Jack! In the flat next door to ours there's an old Miss Rattray, the last of *them*."

Jack had laughed. When he was younger Mum's daft social climbing had made him want to curl up and die, but it didn't matter now. He was eighteen. In July he was off to St Quentin in northern France to work in a hotel for a year, then on to university and the rest of his life. Mum would always talk about "Jack's room," but Rattray House would never be his home.

Jack propped his elbows on the warm sill, closed his eyes and began to count the sounds of summer. The rustle of leaves, the whirr of a lawnmower, the squealing of small children splashing in a paddling-pool. The whack of tennis balls – then, unexpectedly, a song, floating from a window on the floor above. The voice was young and male, and although he preferred more modern music Jack listened with pleasure to the plaintive words and tune.

"*There's a long, long trail a-winding,*
Into the land of my dreams,

Where the nightingales are singing
And a white moon beams.
There's a long, long night of waiting,
Until my dreams all come true . . . "

First World War, thought Jack, who had once done a history project on the subject. 1914–1918. He'd heard soldiers singing that song on a tape.

The notes died away and Jack drew in his head. The smell was revolting, but just as he was opening the door he was again surprised, this time by a loud bugle call nearby. It was familiar to him from Scout camps when he was a kid: *Come to the cookhouse door, boys. Come to the cookhouse door.* Don't tell me Mum's learning the bugle, Jack thought, grinning as he made for the kitchen.

The row about the smell broke out after lunch. Jack tried to raise the matter tactfully but Mum, freaking at the first hint that there might be a niff anywhere in Flat 3, Rattray House, practically shinned up the wall.

"Smell? What smell? Of course there isn't a smell. Trust you to complain about something."

"I'm not complaining. I'm just mentioning the smell –"

"*John!* Come here this minute! Can you smell a smell in Jack's room? See, your father can't smell anything either."

While Mum stood squaring her shoulders like the pugnacious wee Glasgow wifie she really was, and Dad sniffed feebly in the doorway, Jack banged out of the flat in a temper. With fists clenched in his pockets, he stumped down the drive and walked moodily along the verge of the main road. What was it with Mum? he wondered sullenly. Why the hell didn't she just admit there was a stink and get something done about it? As for poor old Dad, nodding and agreeing with everything she said . . . Jack was on his way back, kicking stones and totting up the days till he could leave, when he heard the bugle again. Which was when things really started to turn weird.

The first thing that Jack noticed as he turned the corner of the drive was that the cars – several hatchbacks and a red Range Rover – which had been parked in front of the grey, castellated house were now gone. Instead, standing on the semicircle of gravel before the main door was a horse-drawn wagon, a bit like the ones in western films except that this one had a red cross on its white hood. But that wasn't all.

On the lawn, where two great beeches stippled the sunlit grass with gentle shadow, a table had been spread with a white cloth and green china. Around it sat a dozen or so young men in some sort of uniform, blue suits, white shirts and red ties. Jack saw that several of them were in wheelchairs, and standing around were women in long grey dresses, white headdresses and aprons stamped with a red cross. Jack watched them while doves crooned in the branches and laughter was blown lightly towards him across the grass. For a moment he thought it must be a film set, but then without warning he was part of the act. One of the young men at the table waved to him.

"Good afternoon, Lieutenant Rattray," he called politely, and at once everyone else at the table was waving too.

"Afternoon, Lieutenant."

"Lovely day, sir."

"Good to see you out and about."

Jack stared in bewilderment, then waved back and hurried on up the drive. Suddenly he felt a sharp pain in his left foot, slowing him and making him limp. He was very scared, but it was an automatic courtesy to hold open the front door for two men in khaki uniform who were carrying a stretcher through the hall. They didn't look at Jack, but as they passed he caught a glimpse of the patient on the stretcher. He was about Jack's age, with limp fair hair and blue eyes staring out of an ashen, hollow-cheeked face. His body was humped under a red blanket, and just for an instant Jack thought he must be abnormally small. Then he realised – the boy had no legs. In a daze of pity, Jack watched the orderlies manoeuvre the stretcher into the wagon. Then he slammed the door.

Of course it had been some kind of dream, Jack told himself as he sat with his parents in the sitting-room after supper, staring at the television and trying to disregard the nagging pain in his foot. Not a nightmare but a sort of daymare, over by the time he'd hurried up to the flat and peered from the hall window at the empty lawn. Of course there was an explanation; he'd been shattered after a sleepless night on the train from London, and the row about the smell had upset him. The smell was still there, but he hadn't dared to mention it again. Oddly, it wasn't noticeable anywhere else in the flat.

"I think I'll turn in," said Jack abruptly, getting up from the sofa.

The smell wasn't going to go away and he had to go to bed sometime.

"Sleep well, dear," said Mum, without taking her eyes off the television. But, as Jack moved, she glanced at him and added sharply, "You're limping. What's the matter?"

"Dunno. Think I've twisted my foot," muttered Jack, escaping before Dad could wake up and Mum ask more questions.

Back in his room after his shower, Jack opened the window top and bottom and got into bed. Lying on his back, he stared at the narrow ceiling. Three sides were heavily corniced, the fourth plain where a new wall divided a larger room. Through the wall, in someone else's flat, a clock struck ten, and as the last chime died away Jack heard the bugle again ring out through the translucent northern dusk. *Day is done, gone the sun, from the sea, from the hills, from the sky . . .* The weird experience of the afternoon came back to Jack with terrifying force. His foot hurt like hell, and the disinfectant smell was making him sick. Pulling the duvet over his head, he whimpered desolately, like a small child.

Jack didn't know when he'd fallen asleep nor how long he had slept. What was certain was that he didn't wake up in exactly the same room as he'd fallen asleep in. The window was in the same place but was now curtainless, and in the white moonshine Jack saw that the wall against which his bed had stood had disappeared. Now he was in a narrow, iron-framed bed in a large room with seven other identical beds. Each had an occupant. Someone was groaning, and in the bed next to his Jack could make out a young man with bandaged head, pinioned by cruelly tight bedclothes. The disinfectant smell, with its underlay of ordure and blood, was very strong.

Jack was lying flat, but he was aware of a hump in his bedclothes. Exploring with his right foot, he felt his left leg bandaged in an air pocket created by a metal frame on the mattress. Panic seized him. I've got to get out of here, he thought. God help me, I've got to get out.

Levering himself up on his elbows, Jack managed to dislodge the metal frame and get his legs over the side of the bed. But as he stood up, the pain in his foot screamed up his leg, making him yelp and clutch at the bed-head for support. That was when he saw a pair of crutches propped against the wall; swearing furiously, he thrust them under his arms and began to hop unsteadily towards a half-open door.

The nurse erupted in a rustle of starched white linen and billowed towards Jack like a ship in full sail. Her voice was low, bossy and soothing at the same time.

"Where do you think you're going, Lieutenant Rattray? Get back to bed at once. You're still under orders, you know, even if this is your home. No, not one word. Back to bed, sir."

Jack felt a steely grip on his elbow. He was expertly swung around and propelled back up the long room. The crutches cut into his armpits and he cursed mightily.

"Language, Lieutenant," said the nurse reprovingly. Jack shut up, but he felt too ill to struggle. Meekly he allowed her to manoeuvre him back on to the hard mattress. Her strong hands adjusted the metal frame and tucked the bedclothes firmly in. In despair, Jack watched her remove the crutches beyond his reach. "Go to sleep now," she commanded, moving smoothly away.

Then Jack surprised himself.

"Sister!" he barked, and when she turned with a finger to her lips, lowered his voice only slightly. "Why am I wearing these bloody stupid pink pyjamas?"

She had a beautiful smile, he remembered afterwards.

"A gift from the Rattray House Ladies' Support Group, sir," she chuckled. "Pink for officers, blue for other ranks."

She was still laughing as she sailed away from him between the rows of iron beds.

Dad drove Jack to the Health Centre in the morning, Mum being too busy making sausage rolls for the house-warming in the evening.

"Twenty guests including Miss Rattray," she'd tutted,

"and you have to go twisting your ankle. It looks all right to me, but I suppose we'd better make sure."

Wearing a slipper on his left foot, Jack hobbled out to the car. He was in pain, but worse than any physical agony was the fear that he was going mad. He supposed that what had happened last night had been a bad dream, but if so why did his arms and armpits ache, and why couldn't he get the words of that damned song out of his mind?

There's a long, long trail a-winding
Into the land of my dreams . . .

More like the land of my nightmares, thought Jack bitterly.

Dr Anderson was middle-aged and bald, with a small, gingery moustache. Gruffly he told Jack to take off his sock and the slipper. Jack closed his eyes as cold, smooth hands began to flex his aching foot. In the darkness, he sensed a changed atmosphere in the room.

But it wasn't only the atmosphere. When Jack opened his eyes, everything had changed except Dr Anderson's pink, unsmiling face. The clean modern consulting room had vanished and Jack was sitting, dressed in military uniform, in an office with shiny green walls and darkly varnished shelves. He saw enamelled dishes and fearsome surgical instruments on a trolley, and cylinders of anaesthetic on an iron stand. Dr Anderson too was in uniform. He let go of Jack's foot and said unsympathetically, "Get your shoe on, boy."

Jack groped for the slipper but it wasn't there. Biting his lip he pulled on his sock and eased his foot into a highly polished leather shoe. As he fumbled with the laces, the doctor continued coldly.

"There's nothing wrong with your foot, Lieutenant Rattray. Your wound was healed a month ago and there's no

57

reason why you shouldn't go back to France and do your bit for King and Country. I put it to you that you're shamming, sir."

The tone was brutal, and Jack felt a flush running up his cheeks. His heart was pounding and he was almost in tears, but he felt a strange urge to defend himself.

"Colonel Anderson, sir, I don't know what you mean. I'm not a coward." But then he caught the doctor's eye and heard his own voice rising hysterically. "Sir, I don't want to go back. I was at Ypres. It was hell. My sergeant had his legs blown off, and there was this German, sir. He was running towards our lines, and he was screaming. But he didn't have a face."

Dr Anderson had to call Dad in to help get Jack back to the car.

"If you ask me, Mr Rattray," he said quietly, "this boy's been overworking and he needs a rest. Here's a prescription for some tranquillisers. I'll look in and see him at home tomorrow."

Curiously, when he got back, the smell in Jack's bedroom was gone. After two of Dr Anderson's pills, he went to bed and slept for most of the day. At six o'clock he thought he'd skip the house-warming, but then changed his mind. Better to join in than be kept awake by the noise, and lie worrying about the bad dreams he'd been having lately.

So Jack showered and got dressed, then went into the sitting-room. With a glass of lager in his hand, he wandered round chatting to Uncle George and Auntie Lizzie from Cambuslang, his cousin Mandy from Stepps and a busload from the street in Rutherglen where he used to live.

"Hello, Jack, how are you?"

"Great, thanks, Auntie Lizzie."

"Hear you're going to France, Jack. Ooh, la-la!"

"That's right, Mr Barclay. Place near Amiens. Yes, looking forward to it."

Their new neighbour, "Miss Rattray of the shipping family," arrived late. Watching Mum walking backwards in front of her up the sitting-room, Jack went rigid with the old, buttock-clenching embarrassment. He tried to hide behind Uncle George, but no chance. As soon as Miss Rattray was enthroned on the sofa, Mum started screeching like a cockatoo.

"Jack! Where are you? Come and be introduced to Miss Rattray. My son Jack, Miss Rattray. Did I mention that he's off soon to St Quentin in France for a year, before he takes up his scholarship at Cambridge?"

Jack knew his face was scarlet, but he shook Miss Rattray's blue-veined hand and sat down beside her. She was very old, with faded eyes and thin white hair drawn back from a handsome, if skeletal, face. Quaintly, she called Jack "Mr Rattray."

"How interesting that you're going to St Quentin, Mr Rattray. My brother was there, briefly, during the First World War."

"I expect it's changed a lot since then, Miss Rattray."

"Indeed," Miss Rattray agreed, but Jack could tell that her interest wasn't in modern times. She went on rather dreamily. "Did you know, Mr Rattray, that my parents turned this house into a military hospital during that war? So many young men wounded, the hospitals in France couldn't possibly cope. I was only a tiny child, but I remember the soldiers so well in their blue suits and red ties. They tried to be friendly, but actually I was rather afraid of them, especially the ones without legs. They were always singing. 'There's a long, long trail a-winding, into the land of my dreams . . . ' It seems so naive now, doesn't it?

"My brother Jack was wounded at Ypres in 1915, and Papa pulled strings to have him sent back here – though sadly he couldn't pull strings to keep him."

Jack's eyes were burning and his mouth was very dry. But he managed to say, "What happened?" quite coolly.

"Oh, he was ordered back to France in 1916 and was killed at the battle of the Somme," Miss Rattray said with a sigh. But her ancient eyes brightened, and Jack felt her hand lightly brush his sleeve. "Perhaps you might go to the military cemetery at St Quentin," she said, "and visit my brother's grave? Lieutenant Tack Rattray, 9th Battalion, Highland Light Infantry. Take some flowers – I'd be so grateful."

Jack knew that he was nodding and returning her smile. But the sitting-room was receding, diminishing until he might have been looking at it through the wrong end of a telescope. Then it disappeared and Jack, in a khaki jacket, Sam Browne belt and green kilt, was standing on a station platform as the summer night fell.

All around was activity and the smell of fear. To the left, a grim convoy of tanks lumbered blindly along a dusty road. On the right stood a train, its steam engine whistling impatiently while grunting soldiers heaved guns and cases of ammunition into camouflaged wagons. The air was full of noise, bugle calls, NCOs barking orders, the neighing of horses terrified to be led on board, the scream and thud of shells bursting not very far away. Jack saw the silver sky ruptured by streaks of fire, and a river of blood under the setting sun. Then the ranks of the undead came marching with their tin hats and rifles, left, right, left, right. Halt.

There's a long, long trail a-winding,

Into the land of my dreams . . .

As the soldiers were dismissed and began to scramble into carriages at the front of the train, Jack grabbed the sleeve of a man who was barring doors on the trucks of weapons.

"Sergeant," he cried like a lost child. "Where are we? Where are we going? What's that river called?"

The sergeant was old enough to be Jack's father. His face was haggard and unshaven, but his eyes were kind.

"Shellshock, was it, sir?" he asked gently. "You'll be all right soon, you'll see." Then he dragged his tired body to attention, and saluted the pips on Jack's shoulders.

"Where are we? Advance station, St Quentin, sir. Where are we going? Up the line to the front, sir. What's the river, sir? It's called the Somme."

THE CANAL
Hugh Scott

Running in the wood she went, little Isabella, her hair crinkled out behind her with speed. Oh, speedy, she was, so that the boy couldn't catch her as she dodged around the prickly wall of a holly tree.

"Hey, wait, Isabella!" He ran gasping round the holly and stopped with his hands on her shoulders. He smiled through his panting. "You're a fine runner, Isabella." His hand leapt and cracked against her face so *loud* that the birds stopped calling.

"That's for running faster than me. Nobody runs faster than me, and certainly not a girl with hair like corkscrews."

The blow filled Isabella's head so that she hardly understood. Then the pain dropped to her stomach, bending her as if she might vomit on to the boy's brown polished shoes.

His shoes walked out of her sight. She heard their leather soles crunching through leaves.

Then the boy's feet hit the leaves, running towards her, and Isabella straightened, but her head swam emptily, and she sank to her knees.

The feet pounded closer; then silence for half a moment until his hands landed on her back. His weight jarred her against the ground. His feet struck the earth on either side of her head, then sped away.

"Leap-frog!" he yelled.

Isabella lay stunned.

The birds called to her, and she listened to their sharp sweet words, because listening took away the numbness where her chest had struck the earth.

Pain swelled in her cheek where the boy had slapped her. She could feel the pattern of his fingers on her skin.

She rolled on to her back, tears warming her temples until she snatched at them. She stared at leaves cutting the sky into a million pieces.

Suddenly the boy's feet stepped close, silently, and before she could move, leaves dropped from his hand darkly over her face.

Then he was gone, leaving his laughter to mock her.

Isabella sat up, shaking the leaves off her face. She opened her mouth to throw her wickedest words after the boy, but she thought, really, she should go home and leave him lost in the wood.

Maybe he would fall into the canal.

Isabella had never found the canal. Her grandma said it was somewhere, though. Probably filled in long ago with the bodies of dead trees.

"I *could* lose him," Isabella insisted to herself. "It was me that brought him into the wood. He doesn't know the way out."

Isabella used her hair to dry her tears and took two steps towards home, when the boy's feet pattered again, and she shrieked, and he struck her to the ground before she could dodge.

Then he was gone. And Isabella, oh! was face-down, and sobs fled from her chest, for she was shocked at the all-over bang as she hit the earth.

And she lay too long. Too long, because Arnold's brown toecaps arrived close to her eyes. She hadn't heard him coming because of her sobs.

One brown toecap tapped the earth impatiently. "You're not hurt," he told her. "Get up. Get up!" The toecap hooked her shoulder, lifting her savagely, heaving Isabella on to her back.

Arnold loomed, smiling.

He lowered his smile until his nose touched her cheek. She turned her head but his nose stayed on her cheek; and she tried not to breathe his breath.

"I can run faster than you," he whispered. *"Say it!"*

She said, "Mmm!" desperately.

"You'll say it," he whispered against her skin. "They always do. Little kids always give in – if you hit them enough."

He stood up, and more leaves landed on Isabella's face, then Arnold sauntered away, and Isabella allowed her breath out, and she sucked fresh woodland air into her bruised chest.

The sun rested lower among the branches before Isabella could rise. Every bit of her ached. She considered killing the boy. Boys like Arnold needed to be killed, she thought. She wondered why God allowed them to live at all.

She wished she was big enough to knock Arnold's head against a tree.

But the only thing Isabella could really do was run faster. She *would* run.

And leave him lost in the wood.

With the canal somewhere for evil boys to fall into.

But Isabella couldn't run because, though she tried so hard to dash among the trees, though she tried to make her hair crinkle out behind her with speed, a pain in her knee jabbed at every step, so that even walking was torture, and running impossible.

She pulled up her skirt and saw that her knee was swollen. She must have hit the ground very hard.

She limped towards home, listening for Arnold.

She knew he hadn't finished with her. She knew – even though she was so young – that bullies never get done with bullying.

Bullying wasn't like needing a drink of water where you drank a glassful and felt satisfied.

No, with bullying, the first glass only made you need more, so on you went. Bully, bully, bully. Hurt, hurt, hurt. Because bullies are *weak* inside! (So Grandma said. Or Isabella had read somewhere. Oh, who cares how she knew! She knew!) Bullies are weak and try to prove they're strong by hurting smaller kids! You never see a bully tackling somebody bigger, do you?

No, agreed Isabella.

She thought: he's bound to be following me.

Then tears decided they needed out, and crowded Isabella's eyes until she could hardly see. She sniffed as she walked. She listened for Arnold, but sniffing didn't let her listen well. She found a tissue in her skirt pocket and blew her nose until her eyes cleared and she could hear properly.

Then she found a branch.

Hey, longer than herself, this branch, and twiggy, with shrivelled leaves that looked like dead insects. Isabella dragged the branch with her for company.

She thought it might make a walking-stick to ease her knee. She rested against a tree and tore twigs from the branch until it became a stick. The stick was still taller than she was and willing to help, but Isabella – even now – could not run, but she could walk better.

Sunlight turned red behind the trees.

Tree-trunks began to change into things that moved if you didn't keep an eye on them, and branches no longer decorated the air with green leaves, but reached out to touch a little girl when she turned away.

A tree-trunk ahead of Isabella moved and she stopped.

But the tree-trunk was Arnold, humming to himself as if he wasn't lost. He hadn't seen her.

Isabella limped towards some weeds which sprang out of the floor of the woodland like a vast tall carpet. She laid down her stick and crawled among the stiff stalks of the weeds; she drew in her breath sharply as water rose over her wrists.

She thought of backing out from the weeds, and tried – she tried to move one leg back, but the thick stalks shook, and above Isabella the heads of the weeds nodded, murmuring, 'We'll tell. We'll tell Arnold you're here'.

So Isabella crawled deeper among the weeds, and deeper into the water, so that the water nuzzled her elbows, and lapped coldly about her thighs under her skirt.

But she was hidden from Arnold.

And the cold water eased the pain in her knee.

But her wrists soon grew sore with taking her weight.

She couldn't see Arnold, but she could hear his song, his humming as if he was happy.

Here he comes.

Closer. Here he comes round the mulberry bush. So Granny used to sing. Last night, thought Isabella. Last night, Granny sang about going round a mulberry bush.

Isabella heard Arnold beside the weeds, and she looked

over her shoulder, not daring to ease the weight from her wrists, not daring any other movement in case the weeds decided to whisper to Arnold.

She saw Arnold bend and lift her stick. He didn't notice that the twigs had been stripped off it. He swished it. He swept the tops off some of the weeds.

The sun – very kindly – had left greyness among the weeds to hide Isabella, and Isabella thought that Arnold would need to peep in, to see her.

"I see yo-ou!" sang Arnold.

And Isabella's lips stretched wide as if she might cry out. But her eyes told her that Arnold was lying. She could see him easily in the low sunlight, looking towards the trees.

"I know what you're think-ing! You're thinking you'll run away and leave me lost in the woo-ood!"

Isabella wondered fearfully how Arnold knew her thoughts, until she realised that he had lied about seeing her, therefore he was probably lying about knowing her thoughts. Though he had guessed correctly.

Isabella told herself that Arnold really, really should be dead. A liar as well as a bully. God should have more sense.

"But I'm not lo-ost," sang Arnold, "because when you showed off your running –"

"I never did!" mouthed Isabella.

"– I knew I'd have to punish yo-ou! That's why we came into the wood. It was my idea, but you were too stupid to notice. Little kids are always stupid, which is why I can punish them so easily for trying to show me u-up! I SEE YOU!"

And his voice was so sharp that Isabella jumped. The water leapt up her thighs.

"I'm com-ing!" called Arnold, walking away among the trees.

Isabella eased her weight off her hands.

She stood up. Water drained from her legs as she stared after Arnold through the tops of the weeds. He was swishing the stick among the faint grey trees.

He disappeared.

Isabella waded from among the weeds. She looked at their bulbous heads and remembered their name.

"Bulrushes," she said. Then she recalled Grandma's story about the canal, and thought about the water the bulrushes were growing in.

Perhaps this was part of the canal.

Isabella wiped water from her left arm. The sunlight poured warmly across the grass. The sunlight shone pleasantly on something which dangled on Isabella's right arm.

Isabella raised her left hand to wipe the something off, but her hand stopped, for the sunlight showed her that the something was a black worm; a black worm with nasty red markings dangling from her skin.

As Isabella stared in dismay, the worm swelled.

It was drinking her blood.

It was a leech.

Isabella thought of screaming. Her muscles thought of shaking her arm to fling the leech away. Other muscles thought of turning rigid like wood rather than moving and seeing that dangling horror wiggling with its head in her skin. But Isabella allowed herself to do none of these things.

She had to escape while Arnold was among the trees, so screaming was not to be thought of. And shaking the worm off and leaving its head in her arm was not to be thought of (oh, Grandma had mentioned leeches a few times), and standing rigid was not to be considered!

So Isabella walked, trying to be pleased that her knee

was less painful after being in cold water, then she stopped walking and her muscles almost – very nearly almost – turned rigid because Isabella suddenly wondered if this leech was her only passenger.

She looked along and around the arm with the leech; the leech was alone. She looked along and around her other arm – which was without leeches, but her legs had been in water up under her skirt, and she whimpered as she lifted her skirt and stared, and lifted her skirt at the back and peered around to see the back of her thighs – she didn't dare *feel* the back of her thighs, because that might mean touching a leech with her fingers! If there was a leech. So she peered but couldn't see, and she made herself feel – her fingers ready to leap away at the slightest squashy touch of a horrid ghastly black worm with red marks sucking her blood!

But she found nothing.

She stroked her legs more confidently with her left hand, and peered more boldly.

But her only leech was the one on her right arm.

So she walked.

She walked with her arm away from her body so that she didn't have to look at it.

She began to run.

She ran through the grey air until something monstrous crashed out of the bushes beside her and Isabella *did so* scream!

Then she stopped screaming, for the monster was a cow.

Oh, really. A cow.

Isabella had seen plenty of cows in the woods. She smiled through the remains of her scream, finding comfort in the cow's kindly gaze.

Then she looked at her arm, and saw her blood draining freely, the leech gone.

She glanced back and saw the worm, fat as a purse, on the grass, and she leapt at it, forgetting her pains, and squashed it with her foot so that her blood squirted from the leech and made red streaks on the blades of grass.

Then she ran away from the blood.

She forgot that she had screamed on seeing the cow, and that Arnold might have heard.

Arnold had heard.

She knew this the moment the stick entangled her running legs. She felt the skin on her legs dragged into ruffles as the stick tripped her.

She had been running fast, so she fell fast, and hitting the ground sent her mind into a dark place where her pain retreated.

"You're not hurt." Arnold's voice descended into Isabella's darkness. "You're pretending. You're thinking you can jump up and get away. But you've got to say that I can run faster than you. Say it. Say it, say it. *Say it!*"

Hot pain in Isabella's scalp made her open her eyes.

Arnold's fingers tightened in her hair, and he pulled her face round, and his face approached in the fading light, pale as a ghost; and this was a nightmare, thought Isabella, a nightmare with a ghostly boy and a worm. She had beaten the worm. She only had to beat the boy and she could wake up. And Grandma would tell her it was breakfast time.

Then a swift thing descended towards Isabella's face and slapped her.

Arnold's hand was slapping her. His other hand was in her hair twisting her head round, while this hand was slapping her, hurting very much.

Then it stopped hurting.

Though it slapped merrily on. And some child was screaming; using Isabella's throat.

Then the screaming faded, and the slapping vanished away. Perhaps the hand was sore.

Arnold was sitting back looking at her.

"You're thinking you'll tell your grandma." Arnold shook his ghostly head. "She won't find me. I came here for the day in my dad's car. He's in the pub. I'm outside waiting for him now, like a good boy. I'm always good. Ask him. After you *say it*, I'll go to the pub, and my dad will drive me home. Your grandma will never find me."

His eyes wandered all over Isabella. She still lay on her front where she had fallen, with her face pulled round towards him.

"Your arm's bleeding," said Arnold. "I didn't do that. I didn't hurt your arm! You can't blame me! You did that yourself, you stupid little kid!" He hauled Isabella about until she was sitting up.

She saw blood streaming from the wound left by the leech. She saw the ruffled skin on her legs.

Arnold stepped away and lifted the stick.

Swish.

"You'd better say it."

Swish.

"I don't like girls. I think I'll hit you with the stick until you say it, or until you die. It's up to you. It'll be your fault for not saying it. All you have to do is say it. Say it. Go on, say it."

Isabella couldn't remember what she was to say.

Behind Arnold, the cow strolled from the trees. It looked at him as he raised the stick over his shoulder.

Isabella watched the stick swing up.

Arnold brought the stick down, but it hit branches overhead with a startling rattle, so that the cow skittered away, its hooves flicking up grass; but Arnold didn't hear the cow because he was dragging the stick from among the branches.

He didn't see the cow halt, its tail trembling as it dropped dung.

Then the cow trotted towards Arnold.

His arms were still raised when the cow's big square head struck his ribs, and Arnold staggered across the shadowy floor of the woods, and fell.

The cow fluffed its nostrils as if to say, "There now!" Then it wandered off.

Isabella managed to stand. She looked at Arnold lying so white and gasping.

She didn't want to help him.

But she knew she should.

"I'll tell Grandma," she whispered.

But she had to rest against a tree, her head bowed with pain.

When she raised her head, Arnold was walking towards her, holding his ribs.

"So," he shrilled, "you'll tell your Grandma!"

"Only to help," explained Isabella. But she knew Arnold wasn't listening. She walked a few steps away from him.

He picked up the stick.

Isabella shook her head.

This was too much. She really had meant to get help, and here he was, this liar! this bully! bigger than her, lurching nearer, wielding a stick that wasn't even his!

Isabella ran a few more steps, ran raging, raging! that such a horrid person should live! Well, if God had made a mistake, Isabella was going to fix it and tell Him – tell God – later!

The weeds – that is, the bulrushes – were beside Isabella now. She stopped, her back towards Arnold. She knew what to do. God in her head told her what to do to correct His mistake.

She waited until Arnold was close. She didn't look at him. Oh no, she didn't trouble to look round yet. Maybe he was raising the stick to hit her; maybe he wasn't. She would turn at the right moment.

She turned.

Arnold had the stick raised. Oh, awkwardly, because of his ribs. Isabella hopped close suddenly and punched his ribs.

He screamed and curled up, dropping the stick.

She pushed him among the bulrushes so that he staggered into the water and fell with a splash.

Isabella lifted the stick and used it to stir up the mud at the bottom of the water.

Arnold tried to rise, but he clung fiercely to his ribs, glaring and groaning, and it was easy for Isabella to push him down again. With the stick.

She wouldn't go into the water herself.

Not with worms in it.

When Arnold sat up, a leech was attached to his neck.

Another was on his hand, though he hadn't noticed it.

He struggled to stand, but Isabella just pushed him down. Easily.

In the dim light she saw two leeches on Arnold's face. They would be swelling straight away.

If she stirred them up enough with the stick they would get under Arnold's clothes.

She wondered how many leeches it would take to empty Arnold entirely.

Well.

She had plenty of time.

Grandma wouldn't be worrying about her until it got really dark.

NIGHTMARE
Morgan Llywelyn

Something was breathing in the dark.

Peter lay still for a long time, listening. The sound was coming from the far corner of his bedroom, opposite the windows. In that corner was nothing but a straight-backed chair on which he threw his clothes when he undressed. There was no dog in the room, nor even in the house. No creature at all that could be breathing in his bedroom in the middle of the night.

Yet something woke him up. Something that shouldn't be there.

The inhalations were ragged and gasping, the way Peter sounded after he jogged several miles. But the longer he listened, the less human the breathing seemed.

He should turn on the light and see what it was. He was too old to be lying with the bedclothes drawn up to his chin because of some strange noise. If he got out of bed and investigated, he would find it was only one of the normal creaks and groans of an old house at night.

But he didn't turn on the light. He didn't get up, either. Part of him was excited and turning on the light would just spoil the fun.

And part of him – he didn't want to admit this to himself, but it was true – part of him was afraid.

He lay rigid in the bed, listening; starting to sweat.

Maybe this is just a nightmare, he thought. But he didn't believe it.

The breathing continued.

"Who are you?" he finally demanded. Unfortunately his words didn't come out as brave and full of challenge as he intended. His voice quavered, reminding him that it had changed not so very long ago. Embarrassed, he cleared his throat and tried again. "Who are you? What do you think you're doing in my room?"

No answer, only breathing.

Pitching his voice as deep as it would go, Peter announced sternly, "I'm going to count to five and then I'm coming over there. You'd better speak up before you make me really mad."

The breathing became harsher but there was no other response.

Now he had to get up; he couldn't make an empty threat like some little kid. He was in charge here, after all. He had fought for the right to be able to stay by himself, and laughed at Mum when she was uncertain about it. "I'm practically grown," he had reminded her. "I can certainly mind the house for a fortnight."

The last thing Mum had said before she and Terry left was, "You will be all right until we get back, Peter – won't you?"

"He will," Terry had assured her. Then, turning to Peter he had added with a grin, "I won't let her worry about a thing, I know you'll handle any problems that come up just fine. I have a feeling we're going to be great pals, you and me."

Mum had been lonely for a long time, but lately she had started to sing in the mornings as she cooked breakfast, and there was a sparkle in her eyes. When she and Terry had left that morning to go on their honeymoon, she looked positively radiant.

Until that moment, Peter had never realised his mother was a beautiful woman.

He couldn't disappoint her now. He had to deal with whatever this was, so he threw back the covers and reached for the switch of the bedside lamp. But, like the house, the lamp was old and not in good repair. No matter how he thumbed the switch it wouldn't come on.

Muttering to himself, he slid out of bed. Beneath his blue-striped cotton pyjamas his stomach felt hollow. When his feet touched the floor it creaked so loudly he snatched his feet up again and sat perched on the edge of his bed like some great bird. Then he was angry with himself. He felt like a fool.

It was all the fault of the house, of course.

He had disliked the place from the beginning. It was a tired old farmhouse with a roof that sagged in the middle and some sort of dying vine clinging to the gable end like a drowning man clinging to a rock. The paint was peeling and the rooms smelled damp. But when Mum and Terry had brought him out here to see it for the first time, their faces had glowed as if they'd done something wonderful.

Peter, however, had been dismayed. "You're buying a house next to an old *cemetery*? That's crazy!"

"No it isn't, it makes good sense, son," Terry had replied calmly. Peter hated it when Terry called him 'son', but the older man never seemed to notice. "Because of the location we're having to pay less than we would for the same house anywhere else. It may seem sort of shabby right now, but you and I together can fix it up on the weekends. It'll be great, you'll see. Look at all the space we're getting. There are lots of bedrooms, including one . . . " he had winked at Mum, "that would make a terrific nursery. And there's a huge garden. Not to mention quiet neighbours," he had added with a laugh.

Mom had said, "We did so hope you'd like it, Peter." Her eyes had pleaded with him, like a spaniel's.

Digging his hands into his pockets, Peter had scuffed his toe in the dirt as he replied, "Sure, I like it okay. I mean, well, yeah. It's great."

Big ugly barn, he had thought to himself. And I guess Terry will expect me to mow that acre of lawn, too.

What was wrong with the nice little flat in Rathmines, anyway? It had always been big enough for himself and Mum . . . before. Now he was living in a big old house that made strange noises at night.

Terribly strange noises.

A second something began to gasp along with the first.

The breathing of the new one sounded as if it was being forced through a throat clogged with mucus.

"That's it," Peter told the dark room. "I've had enough."

He slammed both feet down on the floor, hard. Then he fumbled in the bedside locker for the electric torch he had put there before he went to bed. This was an old house at the far end of a country lane and it was the season of summer storms. He had anticipated that the electricity might go off at any time, although he had not expected the lamp would fail to work.

As his fingers closed around the hard, smooth cylinder, he was glad he'd had the sense to plan ahead. The torch was a big one, and heavy. Slammed against an intruder's head it would make a good weapon.

Peter took a tentative step forward, his ears straining to detect the slightest change in the breathing across the room. But there was no response to his cautious advance.

He took another step.

A cold draught ran across his bare feet and ankles and sent a shiver up his spine.

Where's that coming from? he wondered.

Expecting rain, he had closed the windows before he went to bed. He looked in the direction of the door and squinted. In the gloom he could just make out the fact that it was standing ajar. Yet he was certain he had closed it. He always slept with his door closed. If the door was open, that could explain the draught.

But what opened the door?

Peter looked back toward the corner which held the mysterious breathing. The darkness seemed darker there and he could see nothing at all, not even the outline of the chair. He seemed to be looking into a yawning blackness that went on and on without end . . .

"Stop that!" Peter said aloud. He was scaring himself and he knew it. There was an electric torch in his hand; all he had to do was turn it on and shine it into the corner. He ran his thumb up the cylinder and pressed the button.

Nothing happened.

He pressed it again, harder. It was impossible that the lamp and the torch both should fail. The torch made a clicking noise but no light appeared.

If anything, the darkness facing Peter seemed to grow deeper.

There was a funny smell, too; an unpleasant tang in the air that made him feel queasy. Suddenly the last thing in the world he wanted to do was to go any farther toward that lightless corner.

But what else could he do? He was equally reluctant to turn his back on . . . whatever it was, and retreat. If he did go back to bed, what then? Just lie there, waiting for whatever it was to come after him?

Or should he try to escape?

Even as the thought crossed his mind; he heard the door creak on its hinges and slam shut.

A draught could have done that, but Peter didn't think so.

Giving a cry of pure terror, he broke and ran.

Three strides carried him to the door. Dropping the torch in his haste, he caught the handle with both hands and almost wrenched it from the wood. For an awful moment he thought the door wouldn't open. Then he felt it yield.

Flinging it wide, Peter raced through and belted for the stairs.

His footsteps echoed hollowly on the wooden steps. Once he almost lost his balance and tumbled head first, but he caught hold of the banister at the last moment. He hardly slowed his pace, however. When he reached the bottom of the stairs he ran straight for the front door.

Here he stopped. And stared. "I bolted that last thing before I went to bed," Peter said aloud in astonishment.

Yet this door too was standing wide open.

For a moment he could not think, could not even move. Someone definitely was in the house. Intruders, burglars, or perhaps something even more sinister. Should he stay and fight? Or go for help?

He wanted to stay and fight. But only part of him wanted that; the rest of him, fortunately, was stronger. Peter plunged through the doorway and down the pathway toward the lane.

He had no real plan in mind, only an intense desire to put as much distance as possible between himself and whatever was in the corner of his bedroom. His bare feet never felt the stones in the path.

But, by the time he had gone a few hundred yards down the lane, a different sort of stone caught his attention. He was running past the old graveyard that lay beyond the house. The lopsided grin of a half-moon leered over the scene, outlining broken tombstones that emerged like rows of rotten teeth from the mossy earth. Gradually Peter slowed to a walk. His heart was still hammering, but at least he was a safe distance from the house and, as far as he could tell, nothing was chasing him.

He began to feel a little foolish again.

Maybe it had been nothing more than rats. Rats and draughts. Or even just a bad dream.

He walked on slowly, gazing toward the graveyard.

All those dead people. Lives over, futures cancelled. Nothing to look forward to any more. What would they give to be able to have a second chance, to be alive again as he was?

The worn tombstones began to have a strange effect on Peter. Instead of feeling a hushed awe, perversely he wanted to whistle and shout, laugh out loud and throw rocks and make as much noise as one boy, one living boy, possibly could. He wanted to defy death and fear darkness. There was nothing to be scared of, just a lot of broken teeth in the moonlight.

He stopped walking and stood in the middle of the lane. "Stupid," he said aloud. "Stupid, stupid, to be run out of the house like some little kid by my own imagination."

What would Mum say? The first time he was left alone he had panicked. He had let her down, and himself as well.

She and Terry had only been gone for a day and here he was practically wetting himself in the middle of the road just because he had some silly nightmare.

That's all it was. A nightmare. His warm bed was waiting for him back there, all he had to do was turn around and go home.

Home.

Lifting his chin, Peter turned around and started back toward the house. As he walked, a hundred thoughts chased themselves through his head. He'd been resenting Terry, but maybe that was a mistake. Mom was happy and they did have a home of their own now. They were going to be a family.

A real family, with a future. Husband and wife and son, and maybe a baby sometime. A little sister, he'd like that.

And to think he had almost ruined it. What was the last thing he had said to Terry as they left that morning?

"Don't hurry back," Peter had hissed under his breath so low that only Mum's new husband could hear. Then the car door slammed and, as it drove off, he had stood in front of the house, waving, and saying aloud although Terry could no longer hear him, "You don't have to come back at all as far as I'm concerned."

He had meant it just then. But he didn't mean it now.

He was so preoccupied he did not hear the car drive up behind him until a man's voice called gently, "Are you all right, son?"

Peter whirled around, half expecting to find Terry sitting in the car and grinning out at him. But it wasn't Terry. It was a police car with two strange men in it. One of them got out and came toward him.

"Are you Peter Ryan?"

"I am."

"Perhaps we'd better go inside, son. We have some news for you."

The man's voice was so gentle that Peter knew at once. He would do anything to keep from hearing what they had come to say, but the two policemen took him inside and turned on the lights and sat him down on a chair in the parlour. Then they told him. Accident . . . car crash . . . both killed instantly . . . so terribly sorry . . .

As if through a roaring fog Peter heard, not the policeman's words, but the very last thing his mother had said to him. He'd been wrong, it wasn't, "You will be all right, Peter, won't you?"

Just before the car that would kill them drove away, she had leaned toward him with that radiant, happy smile, and said, "We'll come back to you, Peter, I promise. We'll always come back to you."

With dawning horror Peter looked past the policemen toward the stairs. And his bedroom. And whatever waited in the corner.

THE WORM TURNS

Vincent Banville

Harry Masson and James Kilroy were both born on the same day into adjoining houses on Vavaseur Square. The year was 1938, the month August, the town Melford on the backside of Ireland. They were healthy babies, although Harry's mother had a hard time giving birth to him, the consequence being that she slowly faded into a semi-permanent state of invalidism.

The town was coastal, with a formerly fine deep harbour that had now silted up and become non-navigable for bigger ships of the line – the line being the Melford White Goose Maritime Company, owned by the wealthy Swopford family. Many of the men of the town lost their jobs because of the silting up of the harbour and the fact that ships could not get in to unload their various cargoes.

Harold Masson senior was one such who, when he found himself idle, signed up as a merchant seaman, enjoyed a few months of solitude on the high seas and was lost when the 10,000-ton *Kerlogue* was torpedoed by a German U-boat in the North Sea. This happened in 1940, when his only son, Harry, was two years old and his wife, Gladys, was retreating more and more into her spiritual loneliness.

Even at such an early age the two boys, Harry and James, were inseparable; with Harry small, bright and darting, and James a large, slow boy, with glowering eyes and a delight in cruelty that manifested itself in many different ways. They were complete opposites but, as is sometimes the case, were bound together by the proximity of their lives, the fact that each was an only child and, on Harry's part, the sheer fear that he entertained for his hulking companion.

James's mother Betty – usually known as Bet – was a small, inquisitive sparrow of a woman, while poor silent Gladys weighed in at close to fifteen stone. Many people of the town believed that the children had become mixed up at birth, for it seemed improbable that tiny Bet could have produced such a monster as James, while Harry's fragility as opposed to Gladys's poundage was more than laughable.

A mystery surrounded the whereabouts of Mr Kilroy, a thin, sallow-skinned man who, when he was still present and accounted for, was always drunk, beat Bet and tormented his large, awkward son. One day in 1948 he went for a walk with James, but only one of them returned. When the boy was questioned, first by his anxious mother and then by the police, he merely mumbled that he had seen nothing, heard nothing and knew nothing of his father's disappearance. When the absent spouse failed to turn up, and some more years went by, the disappearance became just another legend of local lore.

The town of Melford and the area around it provided ample scope for activity and adventure to the two growing boys. There was the wooden boardwalk that ran along by the sea, and the crescent of concrete bulwark where they could fish for crabs in summer and run from the spuming spray of crashing waves in winter. Old retired sailors had innumerable tales to tell: of two-masted brigantines tacking into the storms of the Bay of Biscay, of phosphorescence like green worms coiling about the rigging, of dead men with gaping eye-sockets surfacing in calm seas, of the doldrums when no wind blew and the air was like fire in the lungs.

Harry's favourite stories were of foreign places and the people who lived there, of Caracas and Montevideo in South America, Mombasa, Dar-es-Salaam, and Cape Town in Africa, while James liked to hear of the hunting of giant turtles, dolphins and whales and the butchering that went on, with the men slipping and sliding in the entrails, and the decks running red with blood.

One summer Harry, going without shoes as was his wont, was impaled by a large splinter from the wooden walkway. It went through the ball of his foot, just behind his big toe, and protruded as a glistening spike in the middle of his sole. James carried him home on his back and then watched with avid interest as his mother, Bet, slowly prised the barb free. The basin of water tinged with Dettol turned red, deeper-hued blood – almost brown in colour – gouted, and all the while James stared, his tongue in the corner of his mouth, his gaze fixed, his attention rapt and concentrated.

Up behind the town rose the twin peaks of Maiden Tower and Three Span Rock, while around them bloomed a wild and wonderful region that children loved to explore. There were gangs from various parts, from High Street, from Temperance Hill, from Fishers' Lane and from Vavaseur Square and, when the weather was in any way clement, they swarmed like ants in, on and about this wilderness of rocks, scrub, ditches and bog-brown streams.

Three Span Rock was easy to climb, but only the more daring attempted the forbidding slopes of Maiden Tower. It was here, in various burrows and caves, that priests hid during the Penal Days, and stories abounded of how they were hunted down by the British authorities and then executed in public by being hanged, drawn and quartered in the town's bull-ring. Many a bold child was frightened into behaving by being told such tales and, on summer evenings when the declining sun painted the tower in hues of crimson and ruby red, it was easy to believe that it was the gore of the slaughtered clerics that was seeping through once again.

Harry would have liked to have been part of one of the gangs, but none of them would take him in because it would also mean having to accept his companion, James Kilroy. Looked on as an ogre and as someone to be avoided at all costs, James cut a lonely furrow and would have been totally shunned were it not for the company of the unwilling, though fixated, Harry. There was a bond between them that even they themselves could not fathom. Like the fly to flypaper, the animal to the trap, the game bird to the gun, Harry could no more escape his fate than sprout wings and fly.

And it was not as if he enjoyed the companionship of his gross acquaintance – in fact, the very opposite. From the beginning there had been an imbalance in their relationship, with James the cruel usurper of Harry's space, mocking and jeering his more gentle preoccupations, teasing him in all sorts of underhand ways, and physically assaulting him when he threatened to run and tell.

Not that there was anyone in the adult world who could help him, for his mother, Gladys, was evermore lost in a shroud of desolation, while the tittering Bet would never believe anything bad of her obese and sulky son. Truly caught between a rock and a hard place, Harry soldiered on philosophically, putting up with the slights, the bullying and the persecution, treasuring his moments away from his oppressor, and pretending an ease of mind that he didn't really feel on the rare occasions his mother roused herself to enquire after his wellbeing.

But then, in his thirteenth year, the Kenny family moved into Vavaseur Square and he met Maggie Kenny and his whole world turned upside down. She was the middle in a family of five boys and four girls, a red-haired, freckle-faced sprite, always in good humour, always on for devilment, always seeking him out and prodding him into laughter, merriment and a sense of the world that was ever of the optimistic, the sundrenched and the true-hearted.

And wonder of wonders, she showed no fear or timidity in the face of James Kilroy's truculence. From the first she took him on as an equal, making fun of his attempts to intimidate her, replying to his taunts in kind, fleet-foot when he resorted to the physical, her quick tongue and laughing eyes serving to slow him down and make him into a buffoon, a shambling ox, a headless chicken.

But he was a dangerous enemy. "Take care, Maggie," Harry warned her as they sat perched on the quaking roof of the hen-house at the back of the Kenny residence and watched the earthbound James shambling about below them, "it's rumoured that he killed his Da when he was only ten . . . "

"His Da was ten?"

"No, James was."

"You're having me on."

"Cross me heart and hope to die."

"So how did he do it?"

"Nobody knows. They went out for a walk and only James came back."

However, the more Harry warned Maggie against

becoming involved with James, the more she took to dogging his footsteps. Because he liked to trap small creatures and then torture them to death, he went out a lot after dark, his favourite stamping-ground being the wasteland of scrub and stunted trees in the vicinity of Maiden Tower. During that summer of 1951, with its sun-bright limpid days and warm velvet nights, Maggie tracked the ill-assorted twosome, tiny Harry and huge James, as they roamed the countryside.

Although town-bred, their frequent forays out of it had made them wise to the ways of the wilderness, and all three of them could traverse rough country as quietly as any of the denizens born to it. In spite of his bulk, James was as silent as a shadow, his disproportionally small feet settling themselves among dry leaves and trailing brambles as lightly as thistledown. He was an expert at setting traps and snares, and the stillness of the night was often broken by the shrill scream of some poor cornered creature. The thrill of the chase always exhilarated Harry, but when the fate of the animal came to be decided – whether it be rabbit, hedgehog, badger or rat – he put his hands over his ears and turned his face away.

If the creature was edible, James would skin it, skewer it on a stick, light a fire in a clearing and roast the carcase. Never one to talk much or to be overly demonstrative, he would smear his face with the blood of the animal, then sit silently with the firelight playing across his painted features. At times like that, Harry could imagine him as being some form of demon, an evil spirit who had managed to free himself from the chains of hell roaming the earth to perform deeds of wickedness.

And it was on one such night that Maggie Kenny inadvertently gave her position away by stepping on a brittle stick. The small snap might have been inaudible to most ears, but James's head jerked up, his eyes glaring in the firelight. As quickly as a breath of wind he was gone, to return almost immediately with the struggling Maggie held firmly in his grasp.

As Harry looked on in fear and trepidation, James bound the girl's wrists together, then looped the cord over the branch of a tree and pulled it taut. Maggie had to stand on her tippy-toes to keep her balance, but fright did nothing to extinguish her courage or the sting of her tongue.

"Let me down out of this, James Kilroy," she commanded, "or I'll tell your Ma and get you a right whipping."

"A whipping, is it?" James growled, his eyes winking like live coals as he glared at the tethered girl.

"What're you going to do?" Harry asked fearfully.

"Watch and learn," James told him, the leaping flames casting crazy shadows across his mottled face.

But Harry, to his shame, cut and ran, tearing his way through obstructions as if they didn't exist, paying no heed to brambles or low-hanging branches, with only one thought in his frantic mind and that was to put as much distance as possible between himself and the scene he could visualise being enacted behind him in the depths of the wasteland.

For a week he cowered in his bed, shaking as though in the grip of a fever. But no matter how he pulled the blankets over his head, news still filtered through to him of the extensive search being conducted for the missing Maggie Kenny. All to no avail, however, for by the end of the week there was still no sign of her, and in the weeks that followed, although her brothers and sisters still continued in their vain hunt, no trace of her was ever found.

When Harry finally emerged from his self-imposed isolation, he was questioned by Maggie's eldest brother, Tom:

"When did you last see her? Where was it? What time of the day . . . the night? What was she wearing? Was she in good form? Bad form? Cheery? Troubled? She was your friend. Surely you must know something . . . be able to help in some way?"

In the face of the barrage of queries, Harry shook his head doggedly and answered in the negative. In his mind loomed the gargantuan shape of James Kilroy, his face streaked with blood, the malevolence in his eyes as he advanced on the defenceless girl – and he himself doing nothing to help, running away from the horror, consumed by fear and shame.

All he could find to say to Maggie's brother was, "I don't know where she is, but I miss her something awful."

The thought of meeting up again with his neighbour gave him nightmares, but when they did come face to face nothing was said, an unspoken bargain seemed to be sealed, and their relationship went on as it always had, yet with a silent screech nail-bitingly just below the surface.

Another year went by, another summer rolled along. Gangs of children continued to use the play area of tangled undergrowth around the twin hills as their playground, while at twilight Harry dutifully followed in the footsteps of his companion, stalking the darkness, the two of them bound together in the terrible breathless guilt of doing bad things.

Until a certain night when they were once again sitting before a glowing fire in the depths of the wasteland, the carcase of yet another small animal roasting amid the embers. From the pit of his silence, James suddenly spoke, the words halting as though being forced out of him.

"I killed me Da," he said, the blood on his cheeks glistening as though it were his dead father's rather than the slaughtered animal's.

"I don't want to hear," Harry replied, putting his hands over his ears.

"And the girl, I killed her too," James went on, a note of satisfaction in his tone.

Harry stared at him as though he were seeing him across a chasm. He knew these terrible things already, but now that they were said they had a terrible finality about them; there was no going back. Either he would have to cut himself free or, from now on, he must become a willing partner.

His mind was made up for him. "Show me," he said, sitting up straight, tightening his fists, feeling pressure in his neck and shoulders as though he were in the grip of a mighty hand.

Silently James stood up, then, as quietly as always, slid away into the darkness. Immediately Harry was on his heels, slipping effortlessly through the undergrowth, a pale shadow of the larger shape ahead. The sky was clear and the moon was up; a silvery patina of light turning everything into a sheen of water-glint. And they were indeed like swimmers as they faced into the tangled scrub, their arms breast-stroking trailing limbs aside, their torsos thrust forward, their hips waggling against the pull of the waist-high foliage. Harry, his heart hammering, followed James's progress as closely as he could, and it was soon borne in on him that they were moving towards the dark and definite shape of Maiden Tower, where it pointed like an admonishing finger into the night sky.

When they got there they paused, then suddenly James disappeared. One moment he was clearly visible in the moonlight, the next it seemed as if the earth had swallowed him up completely. Carefully Harry moved forward, spied the opening in the ground, and stepped down into it. A huge boulder crouched above him, as though it had been rolled back from the mouth of the cave. He stared at it, gave it a tentative shove, and found it unyielding. If it were to move it would undoubtedly block the entrance, a thought that gave him pause to ponder.

He followed the sounds of James's progress, stumbling in pitch darkness, hitting his shins, falling once and having to restrain himself with a great effort of will from scrabbling back on all fours the way he had come. The passage led downwards, and he could smell the dampness and hear the trickle of water. He had often ventured into such caves in daylight, but going in only a little way. He had a fear of cave-ins and being buried alive, something that James did not suffer from, for he often stayed inside these honeycombs for hours on end, emerging finally dishevelled and sweating but otherwise untroubled.

His courage beginning to desert him, Harry was about to turn back when he spied a glimmer of light ahead of him. He pushed on, not with any great degree of eagerness, but forward just the same. The passageway began to broaden, then it suddenly became a cavern, with silvery moonlight drifting eerily into it from a vertical grill high up on one wall. James was standing just under this slit, his head bowed, staring at a pile of loose rock and debris that was heaped there. The only sounds that broke the silence were the renewed drip-drip-drip of water and a rustling, as though small animals were scavenging about in the furthest corners of the cave.

"James?" Harry ventured, his voice booming and then echoing away into stillness. He moved across the floor and stood beside his hulking companion. "What is it? What's there?"

They both stared at the mass of earth, then James went down on all fours and began to dig in it with his hands. He was like a large dog, snuffling and snorting and throwing the clay back behind him. After a time he stopped, then slowly turned to face the appalled Harry. In his dirt-streaked hands reposed something off which the slant of moonlight glistened whitely. It was a human skull, the eye sockets dark shadows, with what appeared to be a ghastly grin hovering about the rest of its features.

James offered it to Harry, but he fell back, shaking his head.

"I don't want to see, I don't want to see," he repeated, as though it were a prayer to ward off the evil in front of him.

"But they're in there," James protested. "You said you wanted to be shown . . . "

Harry shivered, a chill that he had never before experienced invading his being. He felt part of something incredibly wicked, as though a very devil from hell were whispering in his ear and telling him of deeds too black for human minds to grasp. In an effort to rid himself of the horror, he began to concentrate on the boulder that rose above the mouth of the cave, willing it to tremble, to shake, to thunder down and block this awful place with its grisly secret. He shook with the force of his endeavour and, as he did so, there came a tremendous rumble, a deep reverberation in the earth, and the ground shook beneath their feet.

James gazed at him from his kneeling position, a look of shock on his usually blank features.

"What was that?" he asked.

Harry didn't answer. He felt drained, and he made no

move to follow James when he left the cavern, heading back the way they had come. It was with no surprise, either, that he greeted his companion's return shortly afterwards, nor the information that the boulder had moved, blocking the exit from the cave.

"It doesn't matter," James went on. He pointed at the slit through which the light was entering. "You can squeeze through that and go and get help. Don't tell them anything except that I'm here."

Harry looked at where the haze of milky light was filtering in. He knew he could indeed manage to get through the aperture. A plan began to form in his mind, and to give it shape and substance he conjured up Maggie Kenny's laughing face and youthful form.

"Lift me up," he instructed the watchful James. "I can't reach it without your help. And you'll have to push me through."

James lifted him, holding him aloft but making no effort to place him in front of the opening.

"What's the matter?" Harry asked, sudden fear coursing through him.

"You will come back, won't you?" James's muffled voice came from below him. "You won't forget . . . your friend . . . ?"

"No, I won't forget my friend," Harry responded, and he fancied he could spy an encouraging grin on the imagined glow of Maggie's face.

James pushed him in the direction of the aperture and, after a brief struggle, he got through and found himself lying on the shale-covered slope leading up to Maiden Tower's imposing height. He had never breathed air so sweet, never experienced a night so mellow. In the sky the moon was dipping towards the horizon and a spine of glittering stars had replaced it. He had such an impression of space and emptiness, such a feeling of sheer, undiluted freedom. It was as if a burden that he had been carrying for the length of his young life had slipped from him, leaving him as unfettered as a bird suddenly released from a cage.

Hurriedly he began to gather up the biggest rocks he could find, fitting them into the opening in the ground and packing them in as tightly as he possibly could. The rough shale cut his hands, but he ignored the scratches and scrapes, working on as night retreated and dawn began to break. At first he could hear James's voice rising and falling in a kind of crooning tone below him, but then it died away into silence as though the horror of his predicament were being borne in upon him. He was being buried with the two people he had done to death but, unlike them, he would have plenty of time to think about it.

Harry built a large pile of rocks over the opening, then covered it with loose earth, dead leaves and fallen branches. He stood and listened but could hear nothing. Then he went around to where the boulder had moved and listened again. Nothing. The place was as silent as a tomb.

He journeyed home through the awakening morning, realising with a sudden thrill of joy that this was the date of his fourteenth birthday. He was growing up, reaching out towards manhood. Who says August is a wicked month? he thought, and he went with a hop in his step through the blaze of sunlight into the promise of a glorious day.

RAINBOW DREAMING

Soinbhe Lally

When class breaks for lunch, Sara goes to look at the reef. Some days the swell rises, long and snaky across the bay, then peaks and curls for forty yards before crashing down with a sound like thunder. Other days it hisses gently and breaks with a long sigh. Mike and Sara used to go together along the cliff road to look at the reef, but now Sara goes alone.

Often there are vans parked above the surf. Americans who find Californian waves too crowded, Australians checking out Atlantic breaks.

Back in school, they could see the reef from the big windows on the corridor. "Reef's crankin'," people said to each other as they gathered for class, even though everyone already knew.

Inside the classroom they could still hear it. Surfers sat in the back row. "It's hot, may we open the door?" someone would ask and the teacher would fall for it.

Then they could look right down at the reef, through the window on the other side of the corridor. When the teacher turned to the blackboard they looked at the reef. If someone was surfing out there they could see. When the surfer caught a dream wave and disappeared inside the tube, a deep sigh went up from the back row.

Sometimes it got too much for Mike. He would drop his head on the desk, shut his eyes tight and pretend not to hear when the teacher freaked.

That was before Johnny Goorialla came. Everyone had heard of Johnny Goorialla. He was a sort of a myth, one of those tall stories that oldies tell on competition weekends when the party wears into the night and they get maudlin from too much beer.

Johnny Goorialla was there in legendary '75, the summer of surf dreaming when the surf stayed perfect all summer long. There were still people around who had surfed with Johnny Goorialla. Sometimes oldies like Chunkie would reverently point them out and say, "That guy and Johnny Goorialla, they were soul brothers."

Nobody would guess now that the men they pointed out had ever been surfers. They came on Sunday afternoons, men with grey hair and grey faces, driving prestigious cars. The only sign they gave was the way they slowed down on the cliff road and stared at the reef. Then they revved up and drove away.

There were photographs of that summer of '75, photographs of massive swells crashing on to the reef and surfers doing incredible stunts on longboards, riding tandem, doing handstands and hanging ten. A whole section of wall was filled with them in Chunkie's surf shop. Mike sketched copies of the best waves and he and Sara spent a Saturday when the reef was flat, painting waves all over her bedroom walls.

"Some day I'll do nothing but ride waves and paint them," Mike said, standing back to admire his work.

Sara's mum screamed when she saw it. "The wallpaper! What have you done to it?"

"I pulled it off."

"You what?"

"Now, now, Lou," Hank soothed her, "you must let Sara do her own thing, young people need to find themselves."

Hank was Mum's boyfriend. Hank, that is, as in cowboy. By day he packed delivery vans at a cash-and-carry, but at night he sang. When he and Mum went off in his old pick-up to do a gig back in the hills, Mum dressed in a neat little cowgirl outfit which showed off her legs and Hank wore a Stetson, check shirt and high-heeled boots. His voice changed to a western drawl and his walk became a swagger as he slung on his guitar. On the posters they were billed *Hank and Marylou*. Mum wasn't called Marylou, and Sara didn't suppose Hank was really Hank, but she liked him so she didn't ask. People need to live their dreams a little.

Mike and Sara were checking the reef when they saw the van for the first time. It was a typical oldie van, battered and ancient. Snakes and rainbows were painted on the side and *Goorialla* was written in psychedelic letters in the curve of one of the rainbows. There was no sign of Johnny Goorialla.

"Now you'll see real surf," Chunkie said when Sara bought wax at the surf shop. "It'll be '75 all over again."

"Yeah?"

"Johnny Goorialla's here. It'll be surf dreaming, you just wait and see."

Maybe it was coincidence but early on Saturday morning the reef was barrelling. An offshore breeze lifted spray from the curling crest of the waves and blew it backward, making a haze above the swell.

Sara pulled on her wet suit, packed her long yellow hair

into the hood and was paddling out on the rip before daybreak. Each wave rose terrifyingly to ten foot or maybe more and, when she caught one and had to drop down its face, there was such power beneath her that she was afraid her board would snap in two.

Then the wave curled and closed and she was in the tube for a long, slow eternity. When she rode out the wave crashed on top of her and pounded her till she thought she would suffocate, but she didn't care. She had never surfed such surf except in her dreams.

She paddled back out. Rainbows danced in the spray above the waves and she knew that the sun was rising back in the hills. Then she heard the music. Mingled with the crash of the surf was a deep haunting sound which rose and fell with the gigantic swell of the sea. It followed her as she paddled out on the rip current, repeating the same notes over and over, with a hypnotic rise and fall.

The reef was suddenly crowded. Surfers she had never seen before were outside the reef, waiting for waves. She was puzzled. The strangers were riding on big hulking longboards. Yet they were young. Longboarders were usually middle-aged.

The strangers ignored the perfect conditions for carving and wasted precious waves doing stunts, boardwalking and hanging ten. "Party wave," one of them called out and Sara paddled to join in but, when she dropped down the face and cut back up the wave, the longboarders weren't there.

Male insecurity, she thought. Afraid a girl might outsurf them. She surfed till she was too tired to surf any more. Then she rode in and headed up the rocks.

That was when she saw Johnny Goorialla. He was playing on a pipe almost half as long as himself. She realised that the hypnotic music was the sound of a didgeridoo.

They used it sometimes to give a dreamy effect on Australian surf videos. Chunkie played surf videos all day long in the surf shop. As she drew close to the music, it reverberated in the air as if the earth itself was making the hollow throbbing sound.

Johnny Goorialla leaned against a jagged rock at the foot of the cliff. It could be no one else. He was dark-skinned like the oldies said, with black, tight curling hair and broad flat features. "Hi," he said, pausing in his playing, "you got some nice drops there."

She knew what was coming next. Pat on. "You surf pretty well for a girl."

"You play pretty well for a guy."

He grinned. "Yeah, I play well."

"You must be Johnny Goorialla?"

"That's me. I don't know you."

"Sara." Her eyes wandered to the carved wooden instrument. It was ornamented with intricate representations of snakes and rainbows.

"Ever seen a didgeridoo before?"

"I've seen pictures of them. How come the sound carries out on the sea?"

"Only some people hear it out there."

"What do the carvings mean?"

"They show the Snake Rainbow Goddess."

"Goddess?"

"Of the dreaming time."

Sara touched a carved snake and drew her hand back with a yelp of surprise. She was sure it squirmed under her finger. Johnny laughed softly and put the instrument to his lips. The deep notes echoed and rebounded off the cliff face. His eyes grew dreamy. He didn't seem to see Sara any more.

She shivered. She was suddenly cold and her teeth chattered. "See you round," she said, turning away. The haunting sound made her head swim. It must be how a snake feels when it hears a snake charmer, she thought, as she climbed the cliff path to the top.

On her way home she called at Mike's. "Mike, why aren't you out? Surf's incredible."

"Grounded." The word sounded like a moan.

Sara knew Mike's Easter grades were bad. But grounded, that was unreasonable.

"It's ten foot, you're out of your mind to be studying when it's ten foot," she insisted.

They were interrupted by Mike's dad. Mike's dad is the sort of guy who has it all together, nice job, nice house, nice car.

"Sara," he said sweetly. He was always sweet. "Sara, we'd like Mike to see less of you over the next few weeks. It's important that he does well in his examinations. I'm sure you'll understand."

"Wouldn't you like me to help Mike with his work?" Sara asked. "I got straight As in my mocks."

"We have already arranged grinds."

"Oh, well . . . so long." Sara left. Once outside, she went round to the window of Mike's room and looked in. Mike was alone.

"Come on, Mike, live dangerously."

He shook his head.

In the morning, Sara got up early again and hit the water before sunrise. There were more surfers than yesterday. Even oldies like Chunkie had made it out of bed for a dawn patrol. As the sun rose and made rainbows in the spray, Sara heard Johnny Goorialla play his didgeridoo and she saw longboarders start to catch waves.

"What's going on?" she asked Chunkie when she met him outside the reef? "Are they a club or what?" Chunkie was into longboards. He would know if there was a longboard event on.

"Who?"

"The longboarders."

"What longboarders?" Chunkie asked and suddenly turned away, paddling for a wave.

What did he mean, what longboarders? They were everywhere. One of them even dropped in on her. "My wave, you jerk," she yelled, as she cut across his path and made him drop back off the wave.

The big surf had come to stay. Day after day it crashed on the reef.

"What's all this?" Mum asked when she got a letter from school complaining about Sara's absences. "Where have you been when you should have been in school?"

"Surfing."

"But your exams . . . "

Hank interrupted. "Now, Lou, we must let Sara do her thing. She'll be okay." Hank was right. Between tides, there was lots of time for study.

Mike didn't even have lunch-times any more. His father had arranged extra classes.

"Why don't you mitch off?" Sara urged. "You don't have to do things just because your father says so."

"I do, that's the trouble."

Sara knew it couldn't last. She took off one afternoon when the tide was so low that the jagged rocks of the reef could be seen above the surface. In school they were having history followed by double maths.

She paddled out, caught her first wave and took a sheer drop down the face. Then the crest curled and closed over her. Deep inside the wave she knew that just about now an agonised sigh was going up from the back row, that Mike would drop his head on the desk and the teacher would freak.

She was mistaken about the last bit. Mike didn't hit the desk. He asked to go to the toilet.

"Woa," he yelled, ten minutes later, as he paddled out on the rip.

"About time," Sara shouted.

That evening, the vice-principal phoned Mike's father to tell him that Mike had skipped class. His father guessed why.

In the morning Mike was almost in tears. "He took my board away," he said bitterly.

Sara didn't know what to say. Mike could always borrow her board or someone else's but that wasn't the point. Taking away a surfer's board, that was a violation of the soul. "Let's mitch off all day," she suggested.

"I'm in enough trouble."

"So it can't get any worse, can it?"

"You're right."

They knocked at Johnny Goorialla's van.

"Can I borrow a board?" Mike asked. "My old man's locked mine up."

Johnny opened the door wide. "Come in. Why'd he do a thing like that?"

"He wants me to swot. Be a success, like him."

"But you've got a dream of your own?"

"Yeah."

Sara shivered. It was as if Johnny Goorialla could read people's minds. But maybe not. Maybe everyone has a dream.

Johnny went to the end of the van where several boards

were stacked neatly on a wooden rack. The wood was painted ochre and earth red, with pictures of plants and birds and animals which snaked around the intricately-carved supports.

He took a board from the rack. It was a beautiful board. *Rainbow Dreaming* was painted under the glass of the deck, and a picture of a long snaking wave glowing with rainbows ran its length.

"Can I copy that wave sometime?" Mike asked.

"Sure."

Johnny followed them down the cliff path. He sat on the rock below playing on his didgeridoo and the dreamy sound became part of the surf and the sea, the breathing spirit of ocean, earth and sky.

Mike surfed as if surf was about to be abolished, as if he would never surf again. When the longboarders came he left Sara and joined them, surfing his own style, with power and skill, but sitting outside with them. Sara tried to join them but she could never get close. They were always somewhere else by the time she got to where they had been.

Again and again she tried. "Mike," she called out. He waved and disappeared behind a swell. Longboarders came and went, appearing and disappearing like shadows.

"You," Sara called to a longboarder who drew close to her. He disappeared, but not before she recognised his face. It was a face from a photo of '75. The same face, the same board. She had seen them in an old photo, pinned on the surf shop wall.

But that was impossible. Those photographs were more than twenty years old. Besides, she knew who owned that face today. It belonged to one of the grey men who drove by the cliff road on Sunday afternoons, a grey man with a grey face, who stopped to look at the reef, before driving on.

Another longboarder slid down the face of a wave only twenty yards away. Sara was about to call out to him when he flipped over and executed a graceful handstand. Her voice faltered as she realised that both the board and the manoeuvre were familiar. She had seen them a hundred times. They belonged to another of the faded photographs of '75.

Suddenly she was afraid. It wasn't the spooked feeling she sometimes got when she broke the rules and went out on the surf all alone. This was something different. A fear that gnawed at her stomach and made her head swim.

The music thundered in the sky. A swell caught her unexpectedly and tossed her about like a piece of flotsam. Her arms were weak, almost too weak to paddle. She realised she must get to the shore. As the next wave rose, she mustered all her strength, caught the wave and rode it in.

She could still hear the music. It echoed all around and throbbed inside her head. She wanted to lie down on the wet rocks and sleep but forced herself to keep moving, to escape from the sound which seemed to penetrate her very soul.

"Running away, Sara?" Johnny Goorialla said with a mocking laugh. The sound of the didgeridoo rebounded from the cliff face, although Johnny wasn't playing. "Don't you want to be free?" he asked softly.

"Free?"

"I can set you free. You and Mike. Let your souls wander together in the dreaming time."

Sara felt mesmerised. Her will seemed to drain away from her. Desperately she fought the hypnotic power of the music.

"Free to dream for ever."

"No." Sara said violently. "No, I don't need to. I am free."

She forced herself to turn away. "I'm free," she repeated over and over as she scrambled up the cliff path. The mocking echo of Johnny Goorialla's laughter followed her. Her board felt heavy as lead and the music pounded in her head.

She arrived home shivering with cold, her teeth chattering. "You look as if you've seen a ghost," her mother said. She insisted on taking her temperature and sent her to bed.

Through the night Sara tossed and turned. The waves on her bedroom walls crashed and roared and the haunting sound of the didgeridoo mingled with the wind and the sea.

Towards morning she sank into a deep sleep. When she awoke it was late. She realised, with a sense of dread, that something had changed. Something had changed irrevocably.

Yet everything looked the same. Her room was just as it had been. The bed, the surfboard in the corner, the walls filled with waves. With a start she remembered her dreams. She got up and trembling, looked in the mirror, afraid of what might not be there. Her own reflection looked back. She looked closely. Her eyes looked back at her unchanged. Her soul was still her own.

Then she noticed the silence. There was no sound from the reef. She looked out and saw low grey sky above a flat grey sea. The van was gone. The cliff road was empty.

Mike doesn't surf now. Sara sees him in school but he doesn't sit in the back row any more. "Reef's crankin'," she says when they meet on the corridor and he looks at her blankly.

His grades are good. Sara can see that one day he'll be a

success, like his dad. He'll be one of the grey men who drive prestigious cars, one of the grey-faced men who stop to stare at the reef for a moment, before driving on.

In the night-time she still dreams. The pictures on her bedroom wall crash and roar. She hears a haunting music that rises and falls with the swell of the sea and she sees a surfer ride a long, snaking wave with dancing rainbows.

THE FINAL BUST

Tom Richards

(based on an idea by WR Richards)

The slick, blue Trans Am sports car tears along a Los Angeles freeway at eighty miles an hour. It is five o'clock in the evening. Still bright enough that day, eleven days before Christmas. But the sun is going down. And soon it will get dark. Very dark.

At the wheel of the car is a forty-two-year-old male, Ronnie Johnson. Ronnie has owned the vehicle for twenty-four months. He bought it because he could afford it and because it looked hot. He also bought it because he knew the previous owner. An owner who is now dead . . .

In the passenger seat is Sharon Flink. Sharon is a blond, blue-eyed stunner – and Ronnie has the hots for her. He also gets a kick out of the fact that she is so young. Sharon is only seventeen. They have been seeing each other for three months. Despite their time together, Sharon still doesn't know him very well.

When Sharon first met Ronnie, she thought everything about him was cool – his age, his hot car, his weird friends. Her parents didn't like him, of course. Which suited Sharon fine. And, at first, Ronnie treated her well. He bought her things. Stuff she liked. It was all the more reason to date him. But now, Sharon isn't so sure.

Lately, Ronnie emits a peculiar coldness which she finds terrifying. She lets Ronnie touch her sometimes, but only when he insists. Ronnie wants to touch her more, of course. Much more. But Sharon won't let him. She knows that she is playing with fire.

Sharon also knows that Ronnie is a drug-dealer, which is really the only reason that she lets him near her. Before, she would never have been caught dead with a guy like Ronnie Johnson. But this is not her old life. Like many people of Sharon's age, she has come to believe that her life is worthless. Until three months ago, her life was ordinary, and to her, that meant boring. Boring school. Boring friends. Boring family. And then, she met Ronnie Johnson.

Now Sharon is no longer bored. She has something much more interesting. Drugs.

Sitting in the speeding Trans Am, Sharon Flink is high on hash. She is also scared as hell. She is gripping her seat with both hands, digging her long nails into the fabric cushion. Sharon glares at Ronnie angrily, her stomach full of fear.

"Slow down!" she yells at him. He ignores her. Sharon glances at the quivering red speedometer. Her face furrows. "Please . . . slow down!"

Ronnie grins at her. "What's your worry?" he says cynically.

Ronnie is having fun. He weaves the Trans Am dangerously between other cars on the freeway, delighted with the sheer power that roars out of the 402-cubic-inch engine. Suddenly, he takes both hands off the steering wheel. "Look! No hands!" he jokes menacingly.

Directly in front of them, a truck pulls into their lane.

Ronnie grabs the wheel and hits the brakes viciously. The car lurches forward, throwing Sharon hard against the black dashboard. Ronnie hits the accelerator again, weaving crazily to the left, passing the big Freightliner by millimetres. As they pass, Ronnie shouts an obscenity out the open window. His outburst makes Sharon cringe. She is shaking uncontrollably.

She reaches for the paper bag which lies near her feet on the floor of the car. Opening it, she takes out the hash. Sharon loads a small pipe and lights it, inhaling deeply. She feels the dope working on her, relaxing her. Compulsively, she takes another pull.

The world becomes soft and muzzy, floating gently around her . . . her shaking eases and she brings the glinting brass pipe to her lips again. Her eyes close expectantly as she draws in the sweet smoke . . .

. . . *vrrr* . . . *vrrr* . . . *vrrr* . . . *vrrr* . . .

A strange buzzing sound startles her. She looks at Ronnie. He doesn't seem to hear it. The sound is difficult to locate at first, like the sound of an insect flying incessantly toward her . . . *vrrr* . . . *vrrr* . . . V*rrr* . . . VRRR . . . VRRR . . . it seems to move closer to her, rising steadily in tempo.

Sharon still holds the hash pipe to her lips. Her eyes dart quickly around the car, half expecting to see a gigantic wasp or bluebottle banging crazily off the windows.

"What's that noise . . . ?" she asks Ronnie, her voice edged with fear.

"What noise?" Ronnie asks.

. . . *vrrr* . . . *vrrr* . . . V*rrr* . . . VRRR . . . VRRRR . . .

Suddenly, the hash pipe is slapped from Sharon's grasp by an invisible force, hitting Ronnie in the face. He curses as burning ash from the pipe sprays his lap with glowing cinders.

"For chrissake!" he yells. He takes both hands from the wheel and slaps at the bright specks of fire which pepper his jeans. "What the hell did you do that for?" he asks Sharon roughly.

Sharon looks stunned. "I didn't do anything."

"You threw the pipe at me." He reaches out, grabbing her hair with his right hand. "Are you crazy, bitch? You could have killed us!"

"I didn't . . . do . . . anything," she cries again. "Let me go!" She strikes at Ronnie's arm, loosening his grip. Sharon turns in her seat, frightened, searching for the hands that pulled the pipe from her grasp. She stares into the back seat and scans the floor in front of her. Someone . . . something . . . slapped the pipe from her hands. She knows it.

But the passenger compartment is empty. Except for the two of them, they are alone.

"Didn't you hear it?" she says, her voice shaking.

Ronnie glares at her. "Hear what?"

"That sound!" Sharon stutters. "That buzzing sound. It seemed to come closer and closer. Then the pipe . . . something grabbed the pipe." Her eyes are wide, staring at the hash pipe which lies motionless on the car floor.

"I didn't hear a thing." Ronnie watches her carefully. "You should cut down on that crap," he says, motioning toward the hash pipe. "You use too much."

Sharon crosses her arms, trying to hold herself together. She tries not to think about what just happened, about the sound . . . the incessant buzzing sound. Thinking about it terrifies her. She wonders if she is going crazy.

Ronnie thinks that the dope has gone to her head. He thinks she's nuts. He guns his engine, increasing their speed. The blue Trans Am streaks down the Los Angeles freeway, into the coming night.

Two years earlier, Police Sergeant David Corzi drove this same blue Trans Am down this same freeway at a much more sedate speed. Idly, he reached out and turned on the radio. Corzi loved country and western music and now a familiar tune filled his ears. It was getting dark. He should have been on his way home. Instead, he decided to drive downtown to search for a lead to a case he was working on.

Corzi was nothing if not an honest cop. He did his best to protect people and stop crime. Just like it said in the police manuals. And occasionally, he caught a criminal. He would stop a rape. Or bust a drug deal going down.

Corzi liked busting drug dealers best. He had a good reason for it. He hated drugs. Drugs had killed his girlfriend years ago when he was just a kid.

Sandra was a stunner. The original California girl. They met in high school, and kept seeing each other even after he graduated and went away to the university. Corzi would come home on weekends and they'd go out for a pizza, or bowling, or just hang out at her home, listening to Willie Nelson songs on the radio.

Sandra's eyes were always clear and blue. Corzi never suspected that behind those beautiful eyes, something might be wrong.

But something *was* wrong. When Corzi was away from her, Sandra became listless, bored.

To overcome that boredom, Sandra took drugs.

Corzi wasn't with her when it happened. He was at university, in his dormitory room, when the telephone rang. It was Sandra's father. He was hysterical. Sandra had taken an overdose. She was dead.

She was only seventeen.

Corzi never suspected that Sandra had been taking

112

drugs. What he did know was that the only person who had profited from her death was the drug-dealer who had sold Sandra the dope. That's when he started hating drug dealers. That's when the ache started, deep in his belly.

From that moment on, Corzi wanted to protect kids like Sandra from drugs. David Corzi didn't know it, but in losing Sandra he had found his life's passion.

He kept his bitterness intact when he entered the Los Angeles Police Department. With a degree in criminal law, Corzi could have taken a desk job. Instead, he battled the Los Angeles drug rings as if engaged in a personal vendetta. As he grew more experienced, Corzi became adept at uncovering local drug networks. He busted more and more dealers. His boss at the Department noticed. He asked Corzi to go undercover.

Corzi let his hair grow. He wore old jeans and T-shirts. He bought himself a used blue 1978 Pontiac Trans Am. It had a blown 402-cubic-inch eight-cylinder engine. Despite its age, the Trans Am could go from zero to sixty in seven seconds. It was the perfect chase car.

For a year, Corzi drove the blue Trans Am through the burrows of Los Angeles. He'd cruise through the side streets, sniffing out drug deals, and usually there was a bust. Some punk would find himself staring down the barrel of Corzi's Police Special.

And whenever Corzi busted a dealer, he wondered if this was the animal that had sold Sandra the drugs that had killed her.

The Los Angeles dealers came to know about Corzi and his blue Trans Am. Almost single-handedly, he was ruining their business.

In mid-December, 1986 – eleven days before Christmas – Corzi turned the Trans Am off the Santa Monica Freeway, on to Wilshire Boulevard. The street was deserted on that late Sunday evening. It was a dark, brooding kind of night, and Corzi suddenly wished that he'd gone home to bed. Corzi reached down and adjusted the radio. The steely voice of Willie Nelson filled the car. The song's lyrics warmed his soul. It reminded him of Sandra. For Corzi, it was as good as it would ever get.

Then the world exploded around him.

A red Ford zipped out of a side street, pacing alongside him. The Ford's passenger window was down. Corzi could just make out the barrel of a sawn-off shotgun. Corzi's foot hit the accelerator. The Trans Am surged forward, but it was too late. Corzi heard the blast from both barrels . . .

The Trans Am went into a wild side skid. It struck a white and yellow bus stop sign with a thump, broken glass scattering on to the road. The car ploughed on across a cement meridian, sending up a shower of bright yellow sparks. It bounced off a parked jeep, then came to rest in the middle of the deserted street.

The Ford pulled up behind the broken Trans Am. The door opened and a figure with long, black hair and a thick moustache emerged into the darkness. The figure leaned down and ripped open the pellet-ridden door of Corzi's vehicle and stared inside.

Corzi was covered in blood. He moaned – he was still alive. The figure – a local drug-dealer – leaned close to Corzi. The dealer's face twisted into a grin. He grabbed Corzi by the hair, and thrust his lips inches from the cop's shattered face.

"Corzi? You still with us?" he asked.

Corzi couldn't say anything. He felt numb . . . he heard the dealer's ugly laugh. The dealer tightened his grip on Corzi's hair. "You been messin' with our business. You know that, don't you?" He slammed Corzi's head off the steering wheel. Blood splashed thick on the dealer's hands.

The thug stared at the congealing liquid and shook his head sadly. "Messy," he said. Then he looked at Corzi again. "You've been a real bad boy. But I got a little surprise for you. I want you to know something. I knew Sandra."

Corzi stiffened at the sound of her name. The dealer leaned closer. Corzi could smell his rancid breath. "Before I send you to Never-Never Land, I just wanted you to know that I did it . . . I'm the one who sold her the dope that killed her. Just thought you should know."

Corzi's eyes widened; hatred exploded in his stomach. He forced himself to look at the dealer – memorising his face.

The thug moved back a pace. Corzi's eyes followed him. Hating him even as the dealer brought up the shotgun, placing it at Corzi's forehead. Then, the deserted street reverberated with the sound of a gun blast.

The Los Angeles Police Department found the blue Trans Am forty minutes later, David Corzi still in the driver's seat – dead.

Now the Trans Am whips down the freeway into the black night like a bat out of hell.

Sharon is still shaking. The strange buzzing sound persecutes her like a nightmare that won't go away. The buzzing moves toward her, closer and closer, again and again, until she thinks she's going crazy.

With one hand on the dashboard to steady herself, she reaches to the floor of the vehicle and picks up the hash pipe from where it was thrown. She holds it tentatively, wondering if it will be pulled from her grasp again. Sharon loads it with more hash, lights it and inhales deeply, sending her mind to a place as remote from reality as the dark side of the moon. Ronnie glares at her.

"I thought I told you to knock that off," he hisses. When she ignores him, Ronnie strikes out with his hand, slapping her sharply on the side of the head. Sharon cries out, her eyes filling with tears. He strikes her again and again. She feels blood dripping from her nose, and she begins to sob, begging him to stop.

Ronnie grins. "Maybe that's what you need. A little reminder of who's the boss around here." He reaches over, placing a hand on her thigh. He squeezes it roughly and lets his hand linger there. "You like that, don't you, babe?" he asks. His hand moves up her leg as he watches the road.

Sharon tries to push his hand away and sobs, holding her bruised face. She's being punished for her sins, she knows it. She also knows that she shouldn't be in the car. Not with Ronnie Johnson. He could kill her. Sharon should be home with her parents, safe in her bed. She wants to jump out of the speeding car.

From the corner of her eye, she watches Ronnie. He looks like a stranger, and she now wonders why she ever felt attracted to him.

"I think you should take me home," she says.

He laughs loudly, frightening her. His hand continues to stroke her leg. "No way, babe." He winks at her. "Not now, anyway. What say you and me go down to the beach? Smoke some more hash. We'll have a great time."

Sharon shakes her head.

"Look," he says. "You've been enjoying my dope and my car and my money for three months now. You haven't given me much in return." His mouth twitches. "Now *I'm* telling *you* what to do, for a change. We're going to the beach. It'll be deserted. No one will see." He turns to her, smiling. "I won't do anything you don't like, I promise."

Sharon starts to cry again. She feels alone, helpless. No one is here to protect her, not her father, her mother, her friends – she's left them all behind. And now she desperately needs help.

Vrrrr . . . vrrr . . . vrrr . . . vrrr . . .

She hears it again. Her eyes grow wide as she looks around the car and at the still-smoking pipe in her hand. Quickly, she drops it to the floor of the Trans Am.

Ronnie shouts at her. "You're going to burn the carpet, for chrissakes! What did you do that for?"

"Don't you hear it?" she asks frantically. Her head whips around, searching for the source of the noise.

"You're crazy, you know that?" Ronnie says. "Why on earth did I ever get caught up with a kid like you?"

. . . vrrrr . . . Vrrrr . . . VRRRR . . . VRRRR . . .

Now Ronnie hears it. "What's that?"

VRRR . . . VRRR . . . VRRRRR . . . VRRRRRR . . .

Sharon cringes in her seat. She waits, expecting a hand to strike her, like it struck the hash pipe from her grasp.

VRRRR . . . VRRRR . . . VRRRR . . .

Then she feels them – hands touching her. Hands of comfort, not retribution, stroking her softly, gently. She feels a cold energy within them. A power which is suddenly no longer frightening, but protective. Somehow, she feels reassured and she snuggles into the cold hands, as if within her father's warm embrace. The hands tighten around her, holding her gently, yet firmly, to her seat.

Sharon can't move. She should be terrified, but she isn't. Whatever it is has come to protect her.

The radio comes on suddenly. Sharon hasn't touched it, neither has Ronnie. A Willie Nelson song fills the car.

"What the hell?" Ronnie reaches forward, twiddling the dials. He turns it off. Turns it on. Switches to different stations. Willie Nelson continues to sing . . .

VRRRR . . . VRRRRRR . . . VRRRRRRR . . . VRRRRRRRR . . .

. . . Then drumming starts on the roof of the speeding Trans Am. Ronnie looks up in terror. "What's going on here?" He leans forward, staring out of the windshield, trying to peer into the darkness. The drumming becomes a pounding, the pounding a roar, reverberating around the interior of the car.

Ronnie hits the brakes. The tyres lock, skidding on the asphalt of the freeway. The car comes to a stop in the middle of the road. Cars pass them on both sides, their horns blaring . . . inside the car, the pounding stops.

"What was all that about?" he asks, his hands shaking. He looks at Sharon. She doesn't say anything. Her face is calm, almost serene. Ronnie leans over and switches off the radio. The Willie Nelson song dies. Perspiration rolls down Ronnie's forehead. "I've never experienced anything like that before."

Ronnie thinks that it's all over – he wants to think that he imagined it. But Sharon knows differently. Somehow, she knows that it's only just starting.

. . . the sound seems to envelop her, coming from everywhere all at once, surrounding them both . . .

The Trans Am bucks forward. The accelerator is depressed all the way to the floor. Ronnie looks down at his foot. It is planted firmly on the brake. The car shouldn't be moving.

VRRRR . . . VRRRR . . . VRRRR . . . VRRRR . . .

Then he hears it again. His mouth opens in a rictus of terror.

The speedometer creeps up. Forty miles an hour. Ronnie pumps the brake pedal madly. The engine's roar increases. Fifty miles an hour. Ronnie twists the steering wheel wildly to the left. The car fishtails carelessly, tossing him hard against the door. He screams. He lets go of the steering wheel, grabbing his injured shoulder. The car straightens and drives on unaided.

. . . sixty miles an hour . . .

The Trans Am cuts to the right, avoiding a meat truck. The drumming starts again. Pounding all around them. In front of Ronnie, the wheel suddenly spins. The car surges to the left, then the right. The tyres lose their grip on the surface of the freeway. The Trans Am spins . . . Ronnie watches, horrified, as the world spins by . . . then, suddenly, in front of them a concrete pillar rises up out of nowhere. They hit it.

Screeching metal, a shower of sparks. Ronnie pitches forward and his head strikes the windshield. Diamonds of crystal glass shower him, cutting into his face. He screams.

Sharon, sitting beside him, looks on unperturbed, almost as if she is watching a television programme. She is unharmed and she will remain so – she knows it. The hands still hold her gently to the seat . . .

The car backs away from the pillar and rejoins the freeway, rocketing down the lanes. The sky is black, foreboding. Sharon can make out the forms of twisting clouds roaming over the distant horizon.

The car is accelerating. She gazes again at the speedometer. Eighty-five miles an hour. Ninety. Beside her, Ronnie is crying. He struggles to wipe the blood out of his eyes. They feel the wind howl through the smashed windshield.

The Trans Am hits one hundred miles an hour and

keeps going. The freeway curves to the right. Directly in front of them, Sharon can see the concrete safety barrier. Ronnie sees it, too. He grabs the steering wheel, trying to force the car to turn. The Trans Am has other ideas . . .

The car hits the concrete safety barrier at one hundred and five miles an hour. It goes airborne, rotating a full three hundred and sixty degrees, and plummets forty-two feet before striking the empty roadway below it.

Inside, one occupant is tossed about the interior like a broken doll.

Then, what remains of a blue Trans Am comes to a standstill. The broken passenger door opens. Inside, Sharon Flink sits unharmed. The radio speakers crackle. For some reason, Sharon knows what she is about to hear. The voice of the one who has protected her . . . the voice of her guardian angel.

"Get out of the car, Sharon."

Sharon doesn't move. She looks beside her. Ronnie Johnson is still breathing. He opens his eyes, begging for help.

"Get out of the car, Sharon."

She turns, looking for the person who helped her. "You're really here, aren't you?" she asks. The radio repeats.

"Get out of the car, Sharon."

Sharon can't move. Then she feels strong hands pick her up. Lifting her gently away from the car and placing her lightly on the pavement, a safe distance from the wreck.

Now, he stops to look at her – she is so much like Sandra. The pain that she is experiencing is the same. The loneliness. The isolation. The frustrations of growing up. Except, this time, he was there to help.

He turns his attention back to the car. Inside rests Ronnie, the one who killed Sandra. The drug-dealer who pulled the trigger on that December night long ago, ending his physical being – but not his immortal presence. No, not that.

Left to live, Ronnie would be a paraplegic for the rest of his life. It should have been enough. But for David Corzi, it isn't.

Inside the wrecked interior of the Trans Am, Ronnie Johnson cannot move, but his mind still functions; his eyes still see. He can hear and he recognises the voice. The disembodied voice which once belonged to a cop by the name of David Corzi.

The radio crackles. *"Goodbye, Ronnie."*

From his position within the twisted wreck of the car, Ronnie has a clear view of the smashed bonnet. He watches as a small flicker of flame escapes from the hot engine; the yellow light grows brighter, seeking the path of least resistance. Ronnie wills his broken body to flee, but all he can do is watch while the flame moves quickly up the side of the car, towards the pool of petrol which streams from the broken tank.

The quiet night erupts with the explosion. It blossoms brightly in the darkness. Dancing flames quickly consume the car and its occupant. When the fire dies, the world is a little cleaner. A little safer. And Sharon Flink lies unhurt beside the burned-out wreck of the car. Thanks to a cop named David Corzi.

It is his final bust.

THE DEVIL LOOKS AFTER HIS OWN

Rose Doyle

On Tuesday, the second day of Rory Quinn's summer job with his uncle's construction company, the cross was lifted down from over the door of the old convent.

"We can get properly dug in now," his uncle Billy said as it was taken away. "Never like to interfere too much with a place until symbols and such are out of the way."

"Why?" Rory asked. He'd never thought of his uncle Billy as superstitious, nor even particularly religious.

"Better to free a place of its past," Uncle Billy grinned. "The man who owns this place – your boss and mine, don't forget – doesn't have much truck with crosses and the like. He's a businessman, first and last."

"Thought he was the saviour of Ballylee." It was Rory's turn to grin. Charlie Smullen was very rich and very old. When he'd bought the convent he'd announced that his plan to convert it into a hotel and conference centre would put the town "on the map." It was, he said, the fulfilment of a long-held dream of his own.

"Can't do the town any harm, I suppose." Uncle Billy pulled on a cigarette and eyed the drab building in front of them. "The convent was never what you'd call an addition to the town. Unfriendly place, at the best of times."

Rory, hopelessly wishing his uncle would give him a drag of the cigarette, agreed with him. The convent had been closed for longer than his lifetime, which was fifteen years. Over that time the walls had become covered in ivy but remained grim. It would have taken a lot more than a climbing shrub to lend appeal to the unfriendly pile of stone which had housed the convent of the Merciful Good. Rory doubted that making it into a hotel/conference centre would do much for the town, or the building.

Ballylee was a small, quiet place and happy enough to be that way. The biggest change Rory could remember had been the erection of a "Welcome to Ballylee" sign outside the town. Before it went up, cars had driven though without realising they'd come to a town at all. It was Rory's belief that the sign made no difference to this reality. He couldn't see the conversion of the convent changing things either.

"Brew up some tea, there's a good lad," uncle Billy ground the cigarette butt into the gravel with his heel and headed through the convent door. Rory, after a brief contemplation of the raggedy brown remains, decided he wasn't desperate enough, nor so far gone in his addiction to smoking, to try salvaging the fag-end. He went to make the tea.

Tea-making was the single most important part of Rory's job with Quinn Construction. This had more to do with the fact that his yell of "tea's up" signalled a break from work than it had to do with the quality of his brew.

"There seem to be some personal belongings left in the cupboard of the smallest bedroom." Uncle Billy sipped his tea and looked at his nephew. "When you've cleared up here I want you to get yourself up there. Put whatever you find into a plastic bag. I'll decide what to do with them later. Come on now, men, move it . . ."

The workmen finished their break and the sun, fitful that day, went behind a cloud. Rory washed up the mugs and headed for the stairs. The bedroom his uncle had mentioned was at the gable end of the house and was dark as well as small. If it hadn't been for pencils of light poking through the ivy-covered window, he'd never have seen the cupboard, built as it was into a wall. He stood in the middle of the room, blinking as his eyes became accustomed to the fractured gloom, thinking to himself that as bedrooms went he didn't fancy this one at all. It had a musty, unused smell and a dead silence. It was cold too, full of a clingy air which made Rory wish he'd worn more than a T-shirt.

There were marks on the floor where three beds had been crammed close together along one wall. Rory found it hard to imagine three people having room to dress in the space left by the beds.

"Probably tossed for who'd stay in bed and who'd get up first," Rory muttered under his breath. "That's what fellows would have done. But with girls you never know . . . maybe they slept in their clothes."

What he found in the cupboard made this seem unlikely. There were three shelves. Two were empty but the third held a small pile of sheets and thin blankets. Beside them, neatly folded, were four white cotton nightdresses. Rory removed the bedding first and placed it in the black plastic bag. The room became even colder as he worked, the chill seeping into every pore of his body.

"Place needs damp-proofing," his voice sounded small in the silence of the room. "Must tell Uncle Billy there's rising damp in here . . ." he said, an authority after two days on the job. His hand, hovering over the nightdresses in the cupboard, was double chilled by a whisper of cold air. "Must be a loose brick or something in here," he muttered. But it was warm, muggy summertime outside; the air on his hand felt like a sprinkling of frost. He took a quick, firm hold on the nightdresses and lifted them from the cupboard. He felt like a thief, as if he were invading someone's space and stealing their things. A girl's things at that. A girl called Eleanor O'Connor, which was the name carefully stitched into the neckbands of the nightdresses.

"Eleanor O'Connor . . . " he read the name aloud and stopped, disbelieving and fearful, as it came back to him in whispers from the four corners of the room. He tried it again for sound and held tightly on to the white cotton garments as the phenomenon repeated itself and the name again filled the air all around him: "Eleanor . . . anor . . . or . . . O'Connor . . . onnor . . . or . . . "

It echoed and sighed before fading away and leaving the room silent once more. Rory didn't try for the sound again. Hurriedly, he closed the cupboard and turned the rusty key. He stuffed the nightdresses into the plastic bag and wondered as he did so why Eleanor O'Connor's were the only things left in the cupboard. Maybe she'd been rich and hadn't needed them when she finished school. Or maybe she'd left in a hurry or maybe she'd died . . . this last thought made him shudder. Whatever, he'd never know now and he didn't want to.

"You took your time, my lad." Uncle Billy was hassled-looking when Rory got back downstairs. "Leave those by the wall. I want you to help in the sheds at the back."

Mucking out the sheds, Rory forgot all about the plastic bag and Eleanor O'Connor's belongings. It was summertime and he was making money. A dank room and spooky, whispering draughts weren't the sort of things he wanted to think about.

He remembered them that night – or they remembered him. Afterwards, he couldn't quite figure out which way it happened. Whichever, the sighing, whispering sounds he'd heard in the old bedroom woke him from sleep in the dark, lonely hours after midnight. The dark was pitch, the air clinging, exactly as it might be inside a black plastic bag. The whispers were more strident than before and the sound of them filled him with a strange desolation. He sat up and the feeling of fear became stronger. So did the desolation. It clutched at his heart, squeezing until he felt only a hard, aching lump in his chest. He wanted to cry but couldn't and knew, with certainty, that if something didn't happen quickly he was going to drown in unshed tears.

The light came on, almost paralysing him with shock.

"Rory! What's wrong? What's all the banging about . . . " His mother sat on the edge of the bed and shook him gently. It was then he realised he'd been rocking back and forth, knocking the bed against the wall as he did so. He was drenched in sweat.

"Nightmare," he told her. "I had a nightmare." He knew he was lying but there are some things you just can't explain. Not if you don't want to be thought mad. He hadn't had a nightmare. It had been real. Eleanor O'Connor, and whatever terrible thing had happened to her, had been in the room with him. Taking the things from the bedroom cupboard had been a mistake. They'd been left there for a reason and shouldn't have been touched. Tomorrow he would put them right back where they belonged.

Next day, the third of his summer job at the convent, he

arrived early. The plastic bag was where he'd left it in the hallway. He grabbed it and ran with it to the bedroom before Uncle Billy or any of the others could arrive and see him. There wasn't the breath of a whisper from the empty cupboard when he put Eleanor O'Connor's things back on their shelf.

He was making tea a few hours later when Uncle Billy thundered into the room.

"Why on earth is that linen still in the cupboard upstairs? I thought I told you to get it out of there!"

"I did," Rory told the truth before he could think, "or, at least, I meant to . . . " he waffled. As with last night's dream, there were some things you couldn't explain to anyone, least of all to a man like Uncle Billy, he thought, as he trudged downstairs some minutes later with the plastic bag. This time he handed the bag straight into his uncle's hands.

At six, when he was heading for his bike to go home, the bag was where his uncle had left it on the outside steps to the front door. The sky was full of rain, the plastic would never protect the nightdresses. Rory lifted the bag and put it back inside the hallway.

Maybe if he'd left it to become drenched and sodden, the terrors and the chills and the whisperings wouldn't have come back again in the night. Maybe a dose of the elements would have killed the whole thing dead. What was for sure was that when they did come they were worse than before, devouring him to the point where, for an endless time sitting rigid in the dark, he ceased to be a part of the world he knew.

Gradually, he became aware of the chill leaving the room and of scalding tears pouring down his face. He rubbed them with the sheet, soaking it, and lay down, exhausted. But the whispering started up again, at first almost inaudible, then the words slowly became clear and distinctive, the voice clearly a young girl's . . .

"Why me? Why should my life have been made so unhappy? None of it was my fault . . . "

Rory, listening to the sighing end to the question, wondered if he was expected to answer. Before he'd decided, she answered herself. "Innocence is no protection; death has taught me that. But death has not taught me forgiveness, nor brought me peace." This time the pause was longer and Rory shifted uncomfortably. "Will you help me find peace, Rory Quinn?" She asked at last. "Will you put an end to it for me?"

"Put an end to what?" Rory asked, suddenly aware of a silence so absolute he knew she was gone. All at once he was engulfed by exhaustion and fell into a dreamless sleep. He awoke tired and cycled wearily to his fourth day of work at the convent.

"Is that bike of yours in good order?" Uncle Billy asked shortly after midday.

"The best," Rory looked at his uncle cautiously, hoping he didn't want to borrow it. He was very attached to his bike.

"Good. Take this," his uncle thrust a roughly-taped box at him. "There's a few odds and ends from around the convent in there. It occurred to me that old Hannah Murphy in Fineen might appreciate them, as souvenirs of the old place. She worked for the nuns for years, in the kitchen. Seems a shame to just dump them. You know Fineen, don't you? Ask anyone there for Hannah." Without asking, Rory knew Eleanor O'Connor's things were in the box. He hesitated.

"Something wrong?" His uncle looked at him closely.

"No, it's cool," Rory replied.

"Good. No need to come back after. Take the rest of the day off," said Uncle Billy.

Hannah Murphy lived in a stone cottage with a low front door. When she opened it to Rory's knocking, he had to stoop to follow her inside. She was a small woman, round and comfortable and smiling. She was also old and nodded a snow-white head when he told her why he had come. She didn't seem surprised.

"I've no great desire to have souvenirs of that place," she said, "it was never a happy house. But the thought was a kind one. Let me have a look at what you've brought with you."

She gave Rory a glass of milk and biscuits while she emptied the contents of the box on to the table. Rory would have preferred a Coke, but the day was hot and the milk cold, so he sipped it and watched as she took out a couple of framed religious pictures, a jug and what looked like a tea cosy. It was only when she came to the night-dresses that she became at all interested.

"You'd no doubt have preferred Coca-Cola or some such," she said without looking at him, fingering the name on the nightdresses, smoothing them between her arthritic fingers. "Milk's better for you. There's nourishment in milk. Young bodies need nourishment . . . "

Rory, feeling a lecture coming on, stood up to go.

"Stay where you are." The old woman still didn't look at him. "We've things to say to one another." She looked up then, straight at him out of cataractic, tired-looking eyes. They seemed to Rory to see right into him, picking out his innermost secrets. "Where did you get poor Eleanor O'Connor's few belongings?"

Rory told her. "They were the only things in the cupboard," he added.

"They would be." Hannah Murphy fingered the thin blankets. "Not much warmth in any of this," she sighed. "She was a misfortunate creature . . . it's to be hoped she found peace."

"Why shouldn't she have peace?" Rory asked.

"You're young," Hannah Murphy frowned at him, "but you're old enough to know that peace is a gift not given to everyone. The world is full of disturbed souls, both amongst the living and the dead."

"Is Eleanor O'Connor . . . dead?" Rory knew she was – she had to be. Living people didn't invade your head in the middle of the night, they didn't project their terrors so that you almost became what they were – or had been.

"She's dead all right." The old woman's eyes were looking into him again.

"I thought so," Rory said.

"She would have been about your age when she died."

"Fifteen?"

"Fifteen," Hannah Murphy paused. "She died twenty-five years ago, by my reckoning. An accident, they said, but there were whispers too about how unhappy and troubled she'd been and that maybe she'd . . . " Hannah Murphy paused long enough in her story to sigh deeply, " . . . wanted to die. She's been in touch with you, I suppose?" The question was abrupt and unexpected and Rory, taken by surprise, nodded. Hannah looked down at the nightdresses. "So she hasn't found peace, even in death . . . poor Eleanor. There was no one to listen to her, not even myself."

"How did you know she'd . . . been in touch with me?" Rory asked.

The old woman ignored him.

"She came to me in the kitchen one day before she died, but I was busy and had no time for her. I've thought about her manys the time in the years since." She looked up. "*You'll* have to listen to her now, young man, and that's a fearsome responsibility. Whatever uneasy peace she had has been disturbed by the work on the convent."

"How will I be able to help her?"

"You'll have to go through and live her fears with her. You are being given a chance to do great good, an opportunity to help . . . "

"But what about me? Will anything happen to me?"

Miss Murphy hesitated. "You will find compassion," she said at last, "and understanding. Eleanor O'Connor was a gentle soul. She never hurt anyone in life."

Cycling home, Rory made a decision. No way was Eleanor O'Connor getting into his room or his life again. He would talk to her on *his* terms but on *her* territory.

It was a starry night and he had no difficulty getting into the bedroom when he went back to the convent just after midnight. He stood with his back to the wall and spoke aloud.

"I'm here," he said, "so if you've something you want to say then say it. I'm going to stay for half an hour, no longer. After that I don't want you bothering me again – ever. Fair's fair . . . "

Nothing happened. There was no signing, no chilly gusts of air, no whispered words.

"Have it your own way," Rory sank to his hunkers against the wall. "The half-hour begins *now*."

Ten minutes later Rory, cold and impatient, had almost convinced himself that the whole business had been a bout of midsummer madness, when an icy, sighing breath brushed his ear.

"I was your age." The whisper was inside his head and all

around him. "I told Reverend Mother he was going to kill me. She wouldn't listen. She said I was evil and a liar, that my stepfather was a good man and generous to the convent. She locked me alone in this room, night after night, as a punishment . . . " Here the voice rose in pitch until it became a high, thin, unbearable sound. Rory covered his ears with his hands.

"Don't do that." The whisper was in his head. "I want you to *hear* me . . . "

"All right." Rory took his hands away. "Only you'll have to cool it. You wreck my head when you get excited."

A few moments of silence followed. It occurred to Rory that she mightn't have understood him. She'd been dead for twenty-five years, after all. Things were said differently then. But after a minute she went on, her whispery voice a lot more controlled.

"My father died when I was ten and my mother remarried. The man she married was evil incarnate but she, a kind woman, took a long time to see him for what he was. My father had left her a wealthy woman but my stepfather slowly took everything that was hers and made it his own. He insisted I be sent to this convent to board, separating my mother and me in every way he could. My mother couldn't fight him and took to her bed. On my fifteenth birthday, I discovered that he was cheating me too of everything my father had left me. I confronted him. It was a mistake – I knew he would kill me . . . "

"Hannah Murphy said you'd had an accident . . . or maybe not . . . "

"Hannah Murphy . . . " the whisper was thoughtful, "a busy woman. But kind enough. And wiser than most." A pause. "My stepfather is a cruel man. I tried to keep out of his way but he came for me anyway. One morning, when I was home on holiday and thought him gone for the day, I took the dog for a walk along the cliff. He came from nowhere and hurled me over and the dog after me. It looked as if I'd fallen trying to save the dog . . . or as if the dog had tried to save me."

"He got away with it?" Rory asked incredulously.

"He's a clever man. But through the years since, I have known I would be avenged. Just as I have always known he had plans for this convent. He is not the kind to make donations without a purpose. All I've needed was someone to listen . . . "

"Well, you got me. What now?" Rory asked.

"Now you can right a wrong. Charlie Smullen is my stepfather. To you, he may seem an old man intent on fulfilling a dream. In reality he is greedy and evil, determined that every last investment he ever made will bear fruit. I want you to expose him for what he is. Tell the world what he has done . . . "

"No one will believe me." Rory wasn't sure he believed the story himself. The more he thought about it, the more preposterous it seemed. Charlie Smullen, a murderer?"

"You must *make* people believe," Eleanor O'Connor was insistent. "Don't you believe in justice?"

"Of course I do, but . . . "

"Then you must do what has to be done. Only take care. The devil looks after his own and my stepfather has supped long and often with him."

"I'll be careful." Even as he spoke, Rory knew that Eleanor O'Connor was gone.

On Friday, the fifth day of Rory Quinn's summer job and the end of his first week's work, an accident at the old convent shocked the town of Ballylee. It was described in the local paper as "bizarre", "tragic" and "inexplicable".

It happened, the report said, during a visit to the convent by Mr Charles Smullen, the businessman responsible for the refurbishment of the old building. A young holiday worker on the project, fifteen-year-old Rory Quinn, had just presented Mr Smullen with some linen clothing discovered in a convent bedroom. Mr Smullen, clearly moved by the presentation, had accepted and was backing away when a nearby lorry upended its load of gravel. Mr Smullen escaped with slight injuries. Rory Quinn, who had his back to the lorry, died instantly.

THE THIRTEENTH FLOOR
Maria Quirk Walsh

But for a dim glow in the foyer, and the small square of light which shone out from the open lift door on to the corridor of the fifteenth floor, the towering office block was cloaked in darkness. Except for the presence of the night security man, the huge structure was deserted, the staff having gone home hours before. To Martin O'Shea the building seemed even more silent than usual as, stepping from the lift, he stood for a second before reaching out towards the light switch. Pressing it, he waited as the fluorescent tube flickered a couple of times before flooding the area with light. Tonight he felt that even the slight clicking sound it made seemed unnaturally loud in the surrounding stillness.

Martin walked slowly along the corridor, checking that each door was securely locked, while at the same time shining his torch through the glass partitions of the various offices to make sure that no one had been accidently locked in after hours. Or, more importantly, that nobody had gained access without his knowledge. As night security man at the Wolseley Insurance Corporation, he took his work seriously, priding himself on doing his job well, patrolling its corridors at regular intervals. After eighteen months in the position, he still felt a sense of gratitude towards the company which had taken him on, having spent the previous three years on the dole. Now, as he reached the end of the corridor, Martin gave a contented sigh at finding everything in order and, returning to the lift, pressed the button to take him down to the floor below.

Arriving at the fourteenth floor, for some inexplicable reason, Martin's contented mood immediately deserted him. Suddenly filled with apprehension, he gave a slight shiver. He had a feeling that something wasn't quite right and he stood for a moment, listening, before switching on the corridor lights. Outside, a strong wind had whipped up and, as it swirled around the tall building, Martin felt as if the massive edifice had swayed just the slightest bit. Not usually given to such fantasies, he prepared to continue with his round and, glancing up and down the corridor, saw that it was as deserted and silent as one might expect a graveyard to be at midnight. Martin should have felt relieved but, strangely, he didn't. In contrast to his optimistic mood only minutes before, and for the first time in all his nights on duty, he felt uneasy – frightened almost. But of what he couldn't say; there was no one about and, as far as he was aware, he was the only person in the building. Who or what was there to be afraid of? Unable to answer the question, he told himself he was just being stupid. But somehow, no matter how hard he tried, he couldn't manage to shake off the feeling of unease which had taken hold of him, and which seemed to grow with each second that passed. Nor could he quell the niggling memory which began to worm its way to the surface of his mind.

Once again he heard the whispers.

Once again he recalled how, when he'd first come to work for the Corporation, some of the staff members had sent odd glances in his direction as they bade him goodnight each evening. Now, despite his best efforts to block them out, their whispered comments of "Wonder how long this one will last?" or "Bet he'll be out of here in no time, too," began to grow louder and louder until, as he stood there in the huge empty building, they pounded away inside his head. Curious to know what it all meant, Martin had managed to sift a little bit of information here and there, finally piecing it all together. Rubbish, he'd decided then, that's all it was – rubbish! A story which had somehow got out of hand. He laughed sceptically to himself.

But Martin wasn't laughing now!

He was remembering only too well every grisly snippet of information he'd gleaned about that other night security man – of how he'd met his end. Of how he'd taken his own life, of how he had actually hanged himself in this very building only a year or two before. There'd been a time when he too had walked the corridors, walked them just as, Martin was now doing. But above all, Martin was remembering the rumours – that the previous night security man still walked these corridors in a discarnate state.

Perspiring, Martin ran his finger round the inside of his crisp shirt collar, trying to push the unnerving thought from his mind. But, as he continued with his inspection, he unwillingly found himself dwelling on what he'd heard about his predecessor. How, only days before he'd hanged himself, the man had been dismissed when it was discovered he'd been pilfering from the petty cash box. The unfortunate fellow had begged to keep his job, to be given another chance. But management had been adamant, saying they couldn't afford to employ anyone who wasn't trustworthy, especially a security man. The first man to replace him had stayed only a matter of weeks. He'd left without any warning, and no amount of questioning had succeeded in getting a sensible answer out of him. It was clear that he had experienced something he never wanted to experience again. After that, the pattern had been the same, with each replacement staying only a short time and with all of them giving no valid reason for their sudden departures.

But Martin O'Shea had been the exception.

He'd settled happily into the job. Whatever the other men had seen or heard, Martin certainly hadn't experienced anything unusual. And so, by degrees, the whispered comments had ceased and the rumours were gradually forgotten about. Until tonight, Martin thought, as the wind buffetted the building, displaying its powerful strength.

Once again, he questioned himself as to what had triggered this feeling of unease, this apprehension. What had caused these unwelcome, almost forgotten, thoughts to suddenly flood his mind. Things weren't any different tonight to any other night – except that the wind seemed to be making its presence felt more than he'd ever noticed before.

The corridor he'd just walked through was deserted.

The office doors were locked, the rooms empty.

Nothing appeared amiss. What was there to be afraid of?

Nothing, he told himself firmly, straightening his shoulders as he caught a glimpse of his reflection in one of the glass partitions. And so, in control once more, and satisfied that, like the fifteenth, everything was in order here too, Martin once again headed back towards the lift and, switching off the corridor lights, stepped inside.

At the press of a button, the door closed slowly and the lift began to descend. But, after a second or two, the overhead light dimmed slightly and, to Martin's annoyance, the lift came to a shuddering halt. The gauge showed that it was stuck somewhere between the thirteenth and fourteenth floors.

"Damn," he muttered, giving one of the buttons another push.

But the lift didn't budge.

It remained exactly where it was.

Martin glanced at his watch and saw that it was just past three am. What a time to get stuck, he thought. Couldn't it have happened when he was doing his later round, when the staff, the maintenance man in particular, would be in to help him get out? Oh no! It had to happen at this unearthly time of night, which meant that he could be stuck for at least four or five hours!

He jabbed at the button once more.

Again nothing happened.

"Damn," Martin cursed for the second time and, as he spoke, he felt a sudden coldness on the back of his neck. Instinctively he put his hand to it, while at the same time a shiver ran the length of his body. Not for the first time that night, Martin was scared. Something strange was happening, something he didn't understand. And something he didn't like one little bit. Now, too, he had the distinct impression that he was being watched, but from where and by whom he couldn't tell. Slowly he raised his eyes towards the ceiling of the lift, but the vent was securely closed and he found no strange eyes peering through. Still sensing he was being watched, he whirled round to face the mirror on the back wall of the lift.

What he saw reflected there made him gasp with fright.

Standing behind him was a young man, a little taller than himself. His face deathly pale, his skin taut across his cheekbones, with dark circles clearly visible beneath his eyes. His face was expressionless and he seemed to be staring at Martin in a cold, almost unseeing way. His attire, too, made Martin catch his breath, for he saw that the man was wearing a security man's uniform – identical to the one he himself was wearing!

"What the . . . " Martin swung round again, ready to reach out and grab the intruder. But to his amazement, he found there was no one behind him. For a second he couldn't move. He stood as though frozen to the spot. Then, very slowly, he turned to face the mirror again only to find himself once more staring into the same death-like face, the same cold, terrifyingly lifeless, eyes. Martin was petrified with fear. How could he see, clearly reflected in the mirror, a man standing behind him, and yet, when he turned to confront him, there was no one there!

Could he be going mad?

Could he be seeing things which didn't exist?

He had to be imagining this, he told himself, his whole body trembling as, hesitantly, he reached out towards the mirror. When his fingers touched the glass, for one crazy moment he half expected to be able to reach inside, to somehow touch who or whatever it was that was playing this cruel, horrifying trick on him. But his fingers only found a smooth, solid surface. Martin began pounding at the glass, his now damp palms leaving their foggy imprint each time they made contact with it. But his efforts were all to no avail. His tormentor just continued to stand there, unmoving, staring at him . . .

Turning away, Martin frantically groped for the

emergency button, but just as his finger came to rest on it, he felt something being slipped over his head and down around his neck. He grabbed at it and, to his horror, found it was a piece of rope – a noose – rough and tight against his skin. He struggled to pull it off, to wrestle free. But the more he wrestled, the tighter the noose became. In his battle with it, he wriggled round once more to face the mirror, to find, yet again, his white-faced companion still present. But this time, his expression wasn't still and deathlike. Now, the terrifyingly, ghostly apparition was leering evilly into Martin's face, laughing soundlessly at the spectacle of the poor fellow struggling in vain to free himself. Loud, rasping gasps filled the small lift space as Martin, now weakening rapidly, tried to gulp in what air he could, his face puce-coloured, his knuckles white as he grasped at the rope which grew ever tighter round his neck.

But he was wasting his time.

Even as he conjured up every last bit of strength he had in him, Martin knew in his heart that he was no match for this hellish demon. Slowly his gasps grew quieter, his hold slackened until, hands finally falling to his sides, he slumped down, unable to keep up the fight any longer. Just as everything went black before him, Martin let out the most horrible, gurgling sound. It filled the lift area, reverberating off its walls until it found its way out and into the shaft, continuing on down through it, echoing its way into every corner of the dark, empty building. The silence which followed seemed to still even the boisterous wind outside. It was as though the building itself was holding its breath.

And then, a moment or two later, breaking the eerie silence, the lift gave a slight shudder, its light once more coming on full, before it began to make its way smoothly down to the thirteenth floor.

It was 8.30 am when they found him.

The chief accountant of the Wolseley Insurance Corporation was somewhat irritated to find on his arrival that when he rang the doorbell, Martin O'Shea did not make his usual prompt appearance. With a file in one hand and his briefcase in the other, he sighed impatiently as he waited to be admitted. But in the end he had to fumble for his key to let himself in. He walked smartly towards the lift and, looking up, saw that it was stopped at the thirteenth floor.

Must be checking something, he thought, knowing how conscientious the security man was and, pressing the button, watched as the lift made its way to the ground floor.

The chief accountant gasped in shock when the door opened to reveal the body of Martin O'Shea slumped against the far wall of the lift. Hesitantly the middle-aged man stepped inside. Bending down, he took hold of Martin's wrist feeling for a pulse.

There was none.

He looked about the man's head, half expecting to find evidence that he'd been attacked by some intruder or other, but there was no sign of any abrasion, large or small. It was only when Martin's head lolled to one side that he noticed the marks – red weals – as though something had been tightened around his neck. Yet the security man's face was composed, the chief accountant observed. There was nothing in the dead man's countenance which showed any hint of a struggle, let alone signs of strangulation.

Strange.

Very strange, the chief accountant thought as he stood up and left the lift to telephone for an ambulance.

Even stranger still was the fact that, by the time the ambulance men arrived, the red marks on the victim's throat had completely disappeared. They listened patiently as the chief accountant assured them of what he'd seen, anxious to convince them that it hadn't been a figment of his imagination. But when one of the ambulance men pointed out to him for the second time that there were no marks visible now, the poor man had no way of proving that they'd been there, nor any explanation of their mysterious disappearance.

The result of the autopsy was that Martin O'Shea had died of a massive heart attack. Young though he was, the coroner told his relatives, it wasn't unheard of in a man of his age.

On windy days in particular, staff members of the Wolseley Corporation who use the lift regularly have noticed that it seems to shudder slightly – especially whenever it's in the vicinity of the thirteenth and fourteenth floors. The light, too, tends to dim on these occasions. And, for some reason, it always seems to be late evening when these malfunctions take place, as though – as one staff member wryly suggested – the lift, like the employees themselves, tires from its work as the day draws to a close. There have been many complaints about its performance but, despite all their efforts, the maintenance engineers cannot find anything wrong with its mechanism. All they can come up with is that, early in the day, for some reason best known to itself, the lift functions perfectly!

As for the hours of darkness?

Well, of course, no one knows how it performs then, for there's no one in the building at night-time now. Since Martin O'Shea's death, the Corporation has advertised the job of night security man on several occasions, but the vacancy remains unfilled. Surprising as it may seem in this age of such high unemployment, nobody has applied for the job . . .

Also published by Poolbeg

SHIVER

Fifteen ghostly stories from some
of Ireland's best writers

*Discover the identity of the disembodied voice singing
haunting tunes in the attic of a long abandoned house . . .*

*Read about Lady Margaret de Deauville who was
murdered in 1814 and discover the curse of her magic
ring . . .*

*Who is the ghoulish knight who clambers out of his tomb
unleashing disease and darkness upon the world?*

*Witness a family driven quietly insane by an evil
presence in their new house . . .*

*What became of the hideous voodoo doll which
disappeared after Niamh flung it from her bedroom
window?*

Each tale draws you into a web at times menacing,
at times refreshingly funny.

ISBN: 1-85371-300-7